FOX HUNT

A PO SALLY VISION

TWELVE THIRTY PUBLICATIONS, LLC

Telephone: 386.984.2915

Dedicated to my two guardian angels
Sylvonia "Nae Nae" Rich
and
Keira "Stick" Banks
Mother and daughter – gone, way too soon.

SPECIAL THANKS TO
THE BIG HOMIE JOHNNY "BLUE BOY" ROBINSON

Contents

CHAPTER 1

"We have two more, detective." Detective Zy'kia Blunt wiggled free of the yellow crime scene tape draped across the back of his shoulders. Standing within the official crime scene. He turned to scan the crowd of curious onlookers. *Are you the perp?* Zy'kia silently questioned, downloading the features of a middle-aged white male into his memory. His pointed nose, crossed eyes, and bucked teeth, were all stored for future recall. *Maybe it's you?* A muscular black man in his mid-twenties became the object of scrutiny. His low Caesar fade, big owl eyes, and pecan complexion were logged into the space beside the middle-aged white male. *I'll give you a pass pops*, he thought, allowing his gaze to skip over an elderly oriental gentleman leaning on an ivory-handled mahogany walking cane. Its craftmanship was noticeably impeccable.

"These are the fifth and sixth victims in less than a month," a young, uniformed officer stated, leading Zy'kia toward a group of police standing in the distance. Zy'kia swiveled his head, hoping to latch on to any suspicious activity. Seeing nothing that'd warrant an immediate arrest, he turned to follow the uniform.

"Same M.O. as the others, although it is the first time two bodies have been found together. And when I say together, I do mean together!" Zy'kia permitted his eyes to scan the ground while walking in the direction of a white sheet. By experience, he knew, the clue to solving any case could be found where least expected.

"I've seen a few murders in my time," the young cop spoke. "But I do tell ya, this is one to beat all." Stooping to examine a piece of cloth, Zy'kia allowed his gaze to drift to the other officers. By now, they were all intently watching his every move.

They liked to call him Sherlock whenever they felt they were out of earshot. Truth be told, he wasn't only good at his job. He was damn good. In the area of crime-solving, he was unmatched.

Zy'kia removed a pair of tweezers that he kept stashed inside a plastic, dollar store change pouch. Bending, he examined a dirty, grimy cloth closer. The young officer hadn't noticed his stopping and continued walking. Deciding the cloth may be of some value, Zy'kia used his tweezers to pick up and place the cloth into a plastic evidence bag. Glancing up to find the young officer still walking, Zy'kia thought inwardly, *at least now he won't talk me to death before I see the victims.*

"Didn't you say, there were two bodies?" Zy'kia questioned the young uniform. Pointing towards a single white sheet, he added. "Looks like one to me." Several snickers joined the gentle early fall breeze blowing off the Gulf of Mexico.

"There's two, Sh... Zy'kia," Detective Gilmore, Happy as he was known amongst the guys, corrected himself without any harm being done. "We're dealing with a psychopathic serial killer," he paused to point out a Lays potato chip bag mere feet from the white sheet.

"The one thing never mentioned to the press and the one thing consistent at every crime scene. Must be the same guy." They came to a stop in front of the white sheet. "Go ahead. Look."

Zy'kia's eyes rose from the sheet to meet Detective Gilmore's. His mouth opened a split second before his mind opted out of voicing its opinion. Following Detective Gilmore's advice, Zy'kia took the step and a half necessary to get to the victims. Lifting the sheet, he received the unexpected. In nine years of working homicide, he'd thought he'd seen just about all there was to see. It wasn't until this very moment that he knew for a fact that he could truthfully say, he'd seen all there was to see.

A young couple had met their demise while traveling the road to ecstasy. A black male's naked body lay atop that of a white female. The terror-stricken fear stretching her eyes hinted at her seeing her killer seconds before meeting her maker.

"I'd say eighteen. Twenty tops," Happy offered.

"Where are their clothes?" Zy'kia allowed the corner of the sheet he'd been holding to slip from his grasp. The sheet caught on the breeze, exposing a portion of the female's face. One of her terror-filled eyes stared up into nothingness.

"The guy that discovered the bodies, says, there isn't anything different from when he first got here. He called from his cell phone to make sure. Claims he learned that from watching C.S.I. Miami. That's him over there with Curt." Happy pointed across the park towards Curt, his last partner before his promotion to detective.

Zy'kia's eyes followed Happy's left index finger. They stopped to witness Curt talking with an older gentleman of Latin heritage. Curt furiously jotted notes on a pad as the guy's lips moved a mile a minute.

Once his eyes had their fill, he permitted them to fall to the sheet. Seeing the partially covered face, he knelt to cover the bodies completely. "Any time frame of when they were killed?" Zy'kia asked standing to his full six feet.

"Roughly between 8 pm and midnight. They were discovered at 8:30 am."

Zy'kia checked the tried-and-true Timex strapped around his left wrist. A gift from his ex-wife, Kim, for his thirty-seventh birthday.

Five years? Man, time is zooming by. Under the scratched and scarred lens. The hands of the watch read, 8:52 am.

"All right gents! Circle the wagon. If it isn't natural, I want it bagged and tagged," Zy'kia offered motivation.

Four detectives and five uniforms created a circle around the white sheet covering the victims and began the tedious task of searching for evidence.

CHAPTER 2

The ice-cold water pounding his body from the shower head did nothing to quiet the voices tormenting his mind. "I have done everything you've asked of me! What more do you want?" he cried.

He plunged his head into the cold stream, hoping to silence the demons harassing him. "They were innocent. Yet, you insisted they die. I've done my part. Just leave me alone!"

With the turn of a knob, the water stopped its assault. Goosebumps blistered his skin as he reached for a towel hanging over the shower rod. It took five minutes of toweling for a semblance of warmth to return to his body.

Standing in front of the bathroom mirror, he realized Lever 2000 soap washed away the bloody gore manifested by his night's earlier actions, but it didn't touch the feeling of filthiness wearing on his soul. Regardless of how long or much he scrubbed; the dirty feeling remained. It wasn't that he felt guilty for the killings. Remorse was beyond his mental comprehension. After all, it wasn't his fault. The voices were to blame.

Since he was ten years old, the voices had been getting him into predicaments. Old man Jackson's cat was the first of a long line.

At twelve, Auntie Brenda's beloved poodle, Doll Baby. Fourteen, his middle school's mascot, Barbarian the Bulldog. Grandpa Johnson's best milk cow, Beulah, met the voices at fifteen. That's about the time the doctors entered the picture. They'd diagnosed his condition with a word too hard to pronounce, too long to remember, and much too complicated to understand.

Those doctors sent him to another kind of doctor. Psychiatrists, they were called. The dreadful hours he'd spent in chairs and on couches, being asked questions only the voices could answer, flooded from his memory banks.

"Because the voices told me to," he would reply when asked why he did the things he was doing. Soon, the psychiatrist convinced his mother he couldn't function in society, but some doctors could treat him and make him well. She agreed to have him committed to Chattahoochee. Florida's mental hospital.

While in Chattahoochee, the voices were on their best behavior. They were determined to trick the doctors into releasing him, and then he'd make them all pay.

A cheap dime store alarm clock earned its keep. It rang. 7:50 am, time to get dressed and go to the park to see if last night's work had been discovered. Reaching for a pair of worn faded Wrangler jeans, his mind drifted back to the couple he'd stumbled across while they were making love.

At first, he was slightly embarrassed about interrupting the couple's not-so-private, intimate moment. In the next instance, he noticed their differences. His blackness conflicted with her whiteness. Then the voices began.

They must die! The voices screamed.

Sounds of their lovemaking stoked hateful embers, igniting a burning desire to inflict pain. He shook his head violently. Still, the voices continued. Figuring it easier to join them than defeat them, he settled on the conclusion of his life. I must do it because the voices told me to.

Rounding the corner to the park, surprise and displeasure overwhelmed him. There wasn't a soul in sight. Not one squad car that would bring the nosy folks out by the flocks. There wasn't one foot of yellow crime scene tape, to broadcast some sort of tragedy happening. Nothing more than a few early birds searching for a worm, and several squirrels hunting for a morning meal.

In the distance, he recognized the couple exactly as he'd left them. He submitted another tentative glance in all directions as if expecting all he wished for to magically appear. Wish ungranted.

Instead, he was rewarded with a passing school bus. He looked up in time to see a little girl with a smile full of freckles, and her tiny middle finger, extended and pressed against the bus's window.

Dialing 9-1-1, he recalled everything he'd learned from watching C.S.I. Miami. Although he felt positive about not leaving any evidence to connect him to the crime, he checked the area around the bodies again to be certain.

During the night an animal of some sort attempted to rob the scene of the potato chip bag. Using a toe of his dingy, left New Balance sneaker, he nudged the potato chip bag closer to the bodies.

She was a pretty Lil thang, he thought admiring his victims in death. Judging from the intense terror frozen on her features, one might assume her cause of demise to be a heart attack. Which was possible, if that's the effect a syringe full of insulin has on the human body.

Satisfied there wasn't any evidence to tie him to the crime, he concentrated on the 9-1-1 operator. "No one is going to rob me of my glory," he commented after pressing end on the 9-1-1 call. Knowing it'd be a matter of time before he'd be the talk of the town, he squatted on the edge of a merry-go-round to wait for the patrolman that'd be soon arriving.

CHAPTER 3

He gazed over the patrolman's right shoulder, Officer Curtis, but everyone calls him Curt. His eyes came to a rest on a figure that was quickly becoming very familiar. Detective Zy'kia Blunt. He'd learned the name from the articles he'd read in the Playground Daily News. The area's local paper.

Detective Blunt was a twelve-year veteran. Nine of them were spent in homicide. He boasted a seventy-two percent rate of solving the cases to which he's assigned.

Detective Blunt was locally born and raised. A former basketball standout at Fort Walton Beach High School, whose big-league dreams ended with a blown-out knee. Watching Detective Blunt wiggle free of the yellow crime scene tape draped across his shoulders, he began making mental notes.

He didn't focus on Officer Curtis' questions, or the young, uniformed officer standing with Detective Blunt. The detective commanded his full attention.

His heart rate quickened. The young officer pointed in the direction of the bodies and began walking. Detective Blunt followed at a slower pace. His eyes scanned the terrain in search of clues.

"You said, there weren't any clothes when you found them, right?" Officer Curtis' voice shattered his daydream.

Of course, there weren't any clothes! They're trophies. You imbecile, he wanted to lash out. "That's correct officer. They were naked as jaybirds. The way you see them is the way I found them."

Being the first crime fighter on the scene, Officer Curtis had gotten a kick out of the victims getting themselves killed while doing the nasty.

"I thought this type of stuff only happened in Hollywood," he'd stated, staring down at the bodies. "And here I am looking at it with my very own eyes in Fort Walton Beach. Um, um, um. What did you say brought you to the park this morning?" Officer Curtis asked him with his notebook and pen at the ready.

It's a public place you retard! He considered before settling on, "It's my morning routine. I relax in peace and feed the squirrels," he replied removing a bag of sunflower seeds from his right front pocket as proof.

"You think this is the same guy that's been killing lately?" he asked Officer Curt a question of his own.

"No sir. I don't think. I know it is! I hate to say it, but we have a certified crazy, psychopathic serial killer on the loose." Officer Curtis, mistaking anger as fear, added, "Don't worry none. He's gonna slip up. They always do. And when he does…**Bam!**" He slammed his left fist into his right palm. "I'll be right there, waiting gladly to put him out of his misery."

Problem was, it wasn't fear that registered. After leaving Chattahoochee, people made jokes. They called him crazy among other things. The word crazy alone made his blood boil. He wasn't crazy. The voices were.

He looked Officer Curtis squarely in the eyes. Putting on an act like he did to convince the doctors in Chattahoochee of his rehabilitation, he smiled. "Makes me feel safer knowing there's an officer such as yourself on the force." Officer Curtis beamed, as the voices taunted, *KILL HIM! KILL HIM! KILL HIM!*

His eyes left Officer Curtis' right hand jotting his contact information in his notebook, to land on the W.E.A.R. Channel Three news van pulling up. A twinge of excitement coursed through his veins. He'd soon realize the height of his glory.

"That should be all," Curt verbally released him. "If you think of anything else that may be useful, don't hesitate to give us a call."

Walking away, a trace of paranoia intermingled with the fresh release of excitement. *Leave me alone! Stop!* He pleaded with the voices still taunting. Joining the thirty-odd bystanders gathered around, he blended in, becoming just another face in the crowd.

Heads turned as the cameraman spilled from the van. The news reporter walked briskly, hoping to be the first to report this breaking news.

They sped towards the white sheet-covered bodies, while the reporter spoke feverishly into her microphone. The cameraman zoomed in on Detective Blunt and the other policemen canvassing the area for evidence. Evidence one person watching knew was nonexistent.

"All of these killings are ridiculous! We're not safe anywhere anymore!" A female's voice sang out from the crowd.

"I left the big city to get away from this exact stuff. I'll be darn if it didn't follow me from California to Florida," A male offered his two cents.

With the voices relinquishing their mental assault, his heartbeat was at its normal rhythm. *Well, Detective Blunt, the fox lives to be hunted another day*, he said inwardly. *Until the next chase*, he gave a short salute that more resembled him fanning gnats. Turning, he headed for the seclusion and privacy of his small apartment.

CHAPTER 4

From outward appearances, Javid Brown was nothing more than an ordinary Joe. The type you could stand beside without noticing. Which made him exactly whom you wouldn't want to stand beside.

"Seems we have ourselves a serial killer lurking in the shadows. Saw on the news last night where two more bodies were discovered at Liza Jackson Park," the cement truck driver commented while hosing down the truck's chutes. "That makes six murders in one month. Two more than we had all last year."

Second-guessing himself, for providing the police with his contact information, Javid's mind was far from whatever the driver was talking about.

"Prolly one of those dag-born illegals! First the twin towers, now this. Politicians need to get off their assess and build a dag-on wall and keep 'em out for good!" the driver continued, now wrapping the water hose around two metal hooks protruding from the truck's ladder. "Come time I get that .44 Bulldog I've been puttin' off buyin'. Got the perfect excuse now, where the missus can't say no," he added with an exaggerated wink.

Climbing up into the truck's cab, he said. See ya the next time I see ya."

Javid gave a half-hearted wave as the cement truck pulled away from the curb. Mentally, he pondered the idea of moving.

"Why are just so quiet today, my friend?" Poppa, his coworker, and only friend interrupted his thoughts. His Puerto Rican heritage stood out when he spoke.

"Just doing some thinking, amigo," Javid answered, as he used his float to beat miniature rocks under the concrete's surface.

The pair met two years previously. Their most common qualities are what brought them together. New to the area. Poppa from Brooklyn, New York. Javid, Perry, Florida.

Both were down on their luck. Standing at the sign-in desk of Fort Walton Beach's Waterfront Mission, they'd struck up a conversation that has yet to end.

"Tell me ju problem. Perhaps I can be of assistance," Poppa used a trawl to smoothen the cement.

"Aahh Naah, Poppa. It's nothing serious."

"What do you think about the murders? Here, they make a big noise over six people. In Brooklyn, six people die daily."

"I don't think anything about them. We all are dying sooner or later." Javid replied. "Their times happen to come sooner. That's all."

The duo worked at their jobs of finishing concrete while entertaining private thoughts. Five minutes before noon. The driveway was completed.

Javid held a water hose inches from his lips. The water tasted of a rubbery, metallic concoction.

Better for cleaning the tools, he mused after his third gulp. It required another swallow to be convinced of the truth in his thoughts. He lowered the water hose.

"Have you ever wanted to kill? I mean, a person. Another human being," Poppa held his trawl under the stream of water. Dried concrete softened and fell to the earth.

Javid glanced in Poppa's direction. His mouth suddenly felt dry again. Removing the foul-tasting water from the option list, he ran a parched tongue over dry lips.

"Kinda. Onetime," the words were barely out as Poppa blurted.

"Really!? Me too, Papi. I would have done it too, but there were too many witnesses."

Not wanting to entertain this topic, Javid changed the subject by saying, "Well mi amigo. I'll see you tomorrow. I'm going home and wash this mud off me."

"How bout we go for drinks tonight? Pick up some chicas like old times, eh?"

He wants to be a killer and we can use him until he gets used up, the voices all said in unison.

"Not tonight, my friend. I'm tired. I didn't sleep well last night and..."

No!! Tonight! a voice demanded. *You can rest after tonight. Tonight will make us famous!*

"I'll call you before I leave in case you change your mind," Poppa informed.

They finished cleaning their work tools in silence. *Don't let us down, Chip.* The voices used the nickname given by his grandmother when things were serious to them.

You're going out with Poppa tonight. He'll be our scapegoat if we were ever to need one. That's the bottom line.

***

"Hello Happy," Zy'kia rarely used Happy's nickname. Evidence of his calling him Sherlock yesterday, didn't go unnoticed, and now it could be truthfully said. It didn't go unpunished either.

Spinning towards the familiar sound of Zy'kia's deep baritone, Happy couldn't disguise his surprised expression. "Got a minute?" Zy'kia inquired.

"I'll catch you later, buddy," Happy stated, breaking away from Curt. Curt nodded his understanding, waved at Zy'kia, then continued down the hall.

"What's up?" Happy intoned, extending his right hand.

Shaking Happy's offered appendage, Zy'kia replied, "Has our Jane and John been ID'd?"

"As of an hour ago, no. And they don't match any of our missing person reports."

The information struck Zy'kia as being strange. Being as young as the latest homicide victims were, there should have been someone concerned with their whereabouts and well-being, especially after nearly forty-eight hours.

Zy'kia's eyebrows rose slightly and then bunched. The act created a series of wrinkles across his forehead. "What about the toxicology reports?"

"Same as the others. Enough insulin to treat every diabetic in the county. I'm telling you Zy', these murders were committed by the same perp," Happy voiced his opinion.

"A serial killer in Okaloosa County? Never would have thought that. This is a big city's brand of crime. Sure, the Air Force Bases will provide a steady supply of victims. But the area is simply too underpopulated to hide. He has to know: if he stays here. He will get caught." Happy held Zy'kia with his gaze for another heartbeat before continuing. "With tourist season around the corner. I bet the city's leaders are about to crap bricks. You know how they like to count dollars. Only this year they'll be counting lost dollars."

Nodding his head in agreement, Zy'kia changed the subject. "I've been on and off the phone with Captain Winningham, the head of security, over at Eglin Air Force Base. He's offering full support however we may need it."

"You can tell them alphabet boys that we locals are more than capable of protecting our citizens and apprehending a wannabe boogie man," Happy became defensive.

"The cemetery is full of pride, detective. The captain wasn't implying that we were incapable of either. He was genuinely offering his support."

Eglin boasted of being the largest military base in the world, land-wise. It was also Zy'kia's birthplace. Zy'kia's father was a serviceman. Unlike most military brats, Zy'kia wasn't transplanted from country to country, state to state, or even city to city.

His father, a decorated serviceman, earned The Medal of Bravery, The Distinguished Flying Cross, The Purple Heart, and a considerable number of other awards and medals. As well as being an ex-prisoner of war in Vietnam, was fortunate to remain stationed at one base for seventeen years, providing Zy'kia with a sense of stability.

This enabled him to become a basketball prodigy at Bruner Jr. High School. Then propel himself to legendary status while playing at Fort Walton Beach High. Where he earned and signed a full basketball scholarship to the University of Alabama.

Home for summer break at the end of his sophomore year, Zy'kia blew out his left knee during a pickup basketball game. His hoop dreams died two weeks later. Severed by the razor-sharp edge of a doctor's scalpel.

"I don't see how they can help. Even with the government's high-tech equipment. We don't have any suspects. Shoot, we don't even have any clues. All we have as proof are dead bodies. So, unless Captain Winningham and his boys are going to walk the killer through our doors personally. I don't think there's anything they can do." Happy commented.

Zy'kia felt pressured. A self-imposed anxiousness. He'd sworn an oath to serve and protect. Now was the time to do both.

"He'll make a mistake," Happy spoke confidently. "And when he does, we'll be there to nail his ass."

Happy stood peering at Zy'kia. He easily recognized the toll the string of recent murders had on him. Zy'kia's eyes sported dark circles and more bags than a homeless lady. He appeared to be five years older than he was a month ago.

As a way of dismissing Happy, Zy'kia said, "Hopefully, I won't see you before Monday. If I see you sooner…"

He left the remainder of his statement lingering. They both understood. To see each other before Monday, would mean the killer had struck again.

CHAPTER 5

Without a female in the house to complain, Zy'kia often brought his job home. He sat in the den of his house in Northgate Estates. A cold TV dinner sat next to a hot beer. A notebook of facts about the murders commanded his attention.

Zy'kia replaced the chewed tip of a Paper mate ink pen with the lip of his hot Corona. He downed two long pulls, frowned from the aftertaste, then resumed reading the words on paper.

In a quandary, Zy'kia struggled to establish a pattern. He helped himself to another swallow of alcohol, before returning the bottle to his driftwood coffee table. In that instance, his mind danced to memories of Kim, his ex-wife.

She'd purchased the table during the first year of their tumultuous marriage. Shaking his head to clear away the thoughts of her, he concentrated and returned his focus to his notebook.

Six victims. An assortment of races, gender, and age. One Black. One Oriental. Four Caucasians. Two males. Four females. The men were the only non-Caucasians. All they seem to have in common was the way they were killed.

Insulin.

The furthest distance between any two crime scenes was seventeen miles. An indication that the killer used some method of transportation. Then there was the bag of potato chips left behind at every crime scene. One brand, Lays, different flavors.

Uncertain of how, Zy'kia figured the potato chips to be symbolic in some manner.

For the number of crimes committed, it was highly unusual for there not to be a shred of evidence to work from. The killer was careful. Very careful.

Hoisting the Corona to his mouth, Zy'kia's mind drifted to his brothers in blue, most likely gathered at a table in AJ's, their favorite watering hole, downing mugs of draft beer, while acting as though six families haven't been shattered by unexplained, senseless killings.

He traded the Corona for the television's remote controller. With the press of a button, thirty-two inches of modern technology came to life.

He surfed the channels, searching for a western movie. There wasn't one to be found. One glance at his trusty Timex, 9:52 pm, and he readily accepted the fact. This would be another Friday night spent home alone.

***

Why didn't you go with Poppa? Trapped indoors, there wasn't any way to escape the voices. *You know what he wants to do. You're chicken! Scaredy cat. Scaredy cat. Chip's a scaredy cat!* The voices teased.

Either you join Poppa, or we're sending you back to Chattahoochee. To the doctors who call you crazy. To the needles and medicine. To the psychiatrist and their chairs. You're being a bad boy, Chip.

Javid's hands flew to the side of his head. They slammed against his ears. Yet, the persisting voices still penetrated.

Wanna return to Chattahoochee, Chip?

"No!" Javid cried out. "No!" He shrieked. "I'll listen. I promise to be good. I promise!"

Tears rolled from his eyes to bungee jump from his cheeks onto the worn fabric of a hand-me-down sectional.

"Please, give me one more chance. I'll do whatever you want. Please!" He begged.

Oh okay. Stop acting like a wuss. But this is your last chance. I'm warning you. You owe us, big time!

***

Poppa sat in a dark corner inside the Elks Club located on Carson Drive, babysitting a shot glass of 1880 Silver Tequila. His third.

The combination of smooth R & B and alcohol provided the relaxation he now enjoyed. He'd moved on from trying to understand the whys behind Javid not wanting to join him for a night out, especially after he'd volunteered to spring for the drinks. One thing he was certain of, was Javid didn't seem to be himself as of late.

His mind departed from Javid and all his problems the moment she walked into his view. Beautiful didn't properly describe her physical features. She was worthy of masterpiece distinction.

Her hair was cut low. In a style, Anita Baker made popular in the eighties. Her bedroom eyes hinted at untold sensual pleasures, making them more intoxicating than the alcohol in his shot glass.

A small nose sat centered on her angular face. Two dimples accented full luscious lips, that seemed to be fixed in a forever smile. Her jawline hinted of inner strength, strong and sturdy like her chin. The sway of her hips hypnotized Poppa as his eyes escorted her to the bar. She was all he'd dreamed of. Tonight, she'd make his dreams become reality.

Poppa sipped at his drink, studying her intently. He envisioned her pleading, begging for mercy. He felt the muscles in his arms tensing as he visualized her struggling in his grasp. He became mesmerized, one tracked by the possibility of experiencing the power derived from being in total control. The power of determining life or death.

I wish my main man, Javid was here to be a part of my special night. Poppa thought inwardly.

Whenever the thought of committing murder arose, the question of, whether he would be able to take a human life, followed in its wake. Years of internal conversations convinced him that he could.

Poppa leaned forward, propelled by a rush of adrenaline. The moment of truth was surely approaching. A virgin feeling of excitement pulled his lips apart to birth a partial smile. With the victim chosen, Poppa relaxed. He emptied the remainder of Jose Cuervo in his glass, summoned a waitress, and began thinking of a plan.

He immediately dismissed the idea of attempting to converse. Her disappearance was sure to bring investigations. Investigations bring questions. And he didn't want to be the answer to any of the questions. A lesson learned from watching C.S.I. Miami with Javid.

I'll just follow her and ambush her, Poppa decided.

"Tonight's your lucky night," Poppa smiled at the waitress delivering his fresh triple shot of Jose Cuervo with two ice cubes. He liked to joke that one ice cube wasn't enough, and three is too many.

"It seems to be. I'm getting more tips than I've had in months," the waitress replied excitedly.

"Well, add this to your luck." Poppa extended a five-dollar bill.

Snake quick, her left hand struck, nearly faster than the eye. "Thanks!" She beamed, depositing the bill inside her right breast. "Just wave when you're ready for another," the waitress said as a goodbye.

Watching the ripple effect caused by the jiggle her booty cheeks manufactured with every step, Poppa whispered, "It's your lucky night because you were chosen to play the part of the victim. Until the last-minute audition came and stole the role. Perhaps you'll be a star in the future."

Poppa tossed back his drink like a true alcoholic, although he was merely a social drinker. He dared a last glance at his leading lady.

Perfect He surmised silently.

He admired the fact of not being able to see the seat of the bar stool she was perched on. Walking past, Poppa jammed his right hand in his right pocket to camouflage his growing erection.

Sitting in the cab of his Mazda B2000 pickup truck, Poppa waited for the chosen one to bid the Elks Club goodnight.

For fifteen years the truck had been good to him. Loyal in a sense. In return, he did his best to treat the Mazda accordingly. Sure, a paint job and new tires would highly elevate the truck's social status, but under the hood is where it truly mattered, and its engine still purred like a newborn kitten full of tit milk.

Memories of better days filled the cab. Days when he was happily married. In a time before a scumbag, drunk driver ended his fairytale by crashing head-on with his wife and 3-year daughter. They died. The drunkard survived.

He left New York the day he buried them, escaping to nowhere simply running from ghosts haunting him whether awake or asleep. On the verge of becoming emotional, the Elks' Club door swung open. Seeing his prize disengaged Poppa from the past.

CHAPTER 6

"Are you all right ma'am?" Poppa scanned the streets. Empty.

At the red light on the intersection of Jonquil Avenue and Mary Esther Cut-off, Poppa allowed the Mazda to hit the rear of her Acura TL.

"Yes. I'm fine, but... How could you not see me?" Her slurred speech revealed the truth of her maybe having one too many drinks.

Turning on his Latin heritage, Poppa replied. "I see you. It's my foot. It slip off brake and land on gas."

Fuckin' immigrant, prolly ain't got insurance, she declared to herself.

"Perhaps it best we move to that parking lot," Poppa pointed towards the Eglin Federal Credit Union. "Out of the road. Then we can inspect for damage. I give you the paper for my insurance. You car broke. I fix," Poppa attempted to relax her.

She glanced in the parking lot's direction, then down at her watch.

"Okay."

The answer was music to Poppa's ears. His plan was progressing righteously.

Making sure to stay away from the ATM, and the surveillance cameras it demands, Poppa parked.

He was standing at her car door as she opened it. No sooner than her body rose to its full five feet six inches, did Poppa uncork a looping right hand. It was specially made. Backed by every ounce of his one hundred fifty-five pounds.

Landing, the punch sounded grotesque. Bone crashing against bone knocked her out instantly.

21

Poppa caught her as she fell forward. Carrying her, he walked rapidly.

Inside the Mazda, he quickly taped her hands and feet. Then stuffed a handkerchief in her mouth to serve as a gag.

Another detailed glance at his surroundings assured him of no one seeing him act. He released a sigh of relief.

A half turn of the ignition key awakened the kitty from its slumber. Happy to be assisting its owner, the Mazda purred.

On Mary Esther Cut-off without any sign of human life, Poppa celebrated pulling off the hard part without the slightest bit of resistance. The partial smile birthed inside of the Elks Club matured to adulthood.

He looked over at the sleeping figure he'd come to recognize as his prize. Unconsciously, Poppa ran his left hand across his growing manliness. Oddly, his mind drifted to Javid.

He's probably asleep. He concluded the thought by saying, "This could be a C.S.I. Miami episode."

***

Zy'kia sat at the edge of his humongous Tempur-Pedic California king-sized mattress. He yawned to clear the fog from his head, before blinking the red L.E.D. numbers of the digital clock into focus, 4:16 am.

Another body being discovered was to blame for his being awake at this ungodly hour on a Saturday morning.

"A black female. Thirty to thirty-five years of age." Happy's voice rang in his head.

My age, He thought forcing his right foot into a Nike Cross Trainer that didn't fit properly. Yet, its counterpart, the left, fit perfectly.

Apparent strangulation, huh? He questioned the meaning of that information as he slipped a Ralph Lauren pullover over his head. *Either our boy has changed his methods, or we have two killers.*

"Security company found the body," Happy's breath wreaked of alcohol. He'd met Zy'kia at the crime scene's perimeter and began bringing him up to date.

"My guess is, she wasn't killed here," Happy held the yellow tape high enough for Zy'kia to duck under. "She's pretty as pretty gets. I'll give her that much."

They were in the parking lot of the Santa Rosa Mall. In front of the JC Penny entrance. Aside from the six police cruisers, one ambulance, and the three detective vehicles. The parking lot was empty.

Noticing there wasn't a vehicle representing a security company Zy'kia asked, "Where's the person that discovered the body?"

"He's in a squad car. The company needed his vehicle for the next shift," Happy answered, guiding Zy'kia toward the main attraction. A single white sheet.

"There wasn't any ID," Happy spoke as Zy'kia raised the sheet by a corner.

"What the!" Zy'kia exclaimed. "Ah naw! It can't be!"

"You know her?" Happy's tone implied the impossibility of that being possible.

Ignoring Happy, Zy'kia stared down at the features he once fantasized would become those of his wife. Visions of them sitting across from each other in ninth-grade Civics at Bruner Jr. High paraded through his mind. For him, it was love at first sight. For her, he didn't seem to exist.

Still looking down, he answered Happy's almost forgotten question. "Gloria Walters," Releasing the sheet's corner, he turned and walked away.

A full five minutes expired before Happy summoned the courage to approach Zy'kia. "Hey. Are you okay, man?"

"Yeah. I'm good. Just the last person I'd expected. I'm not saying, I expected to see anyone. I'm trying to say, she's the very last person I'd expected. Still isn't coming out right huh?"

"Don't worry. I understand what you mean," Happy provided a lifeline.

"We have to catch this dude," Zy'kia slid off the trunk of the police cruiser he'd been sitting on.

"I'd say, dudes. Nothing about this one fits the M.O. of the others. From the method used, to there not being a bag of potato chips. My money is on there being two killers," Happy commented.

Zy'kia nodded his head in agreement. "The girl. She mean something to you?" Happy asked sincerely.

Zy'kia's eyes revolved to bring the white sheet into view. "Enough to make moving forward personal," He replied flatly.

"We met in Jr. High. Infatuation was my crush, but she didn't speak one hundred words to me before our sophomore year of high school. We took our time, but we eventually got around to developing a decent enough friendship. I haven't seen her in years. The last I heard. She'd married a G.I. and was living abroad."

Because of a long night of hard drinking Happy struggled to find the proper response. The impossibility caused the next two minutes to be spent with them standing behind the police cruiser in awkward silence.

Patches of gray blotted the sky, hinting at sunrise quickly approaching. "If she wasn't killed here, then there won't be much to find as far as clues go. Let's comb the area. I want her body moved before the media arrives. I couldn't protect her, but I can save her the disrespect of being broadcast as just another piece of meat," Glad to abandon the awkwardness of the moment, Happy strode off to relay Zy'kia's wishes to the other officers.

With the sun above the horizon, the parking lot was abuzz with the usual curious onlookers. This group was mainly composed of workers who'd left home thinking they were on their way to carrying out the duties involved in their normal workdays. They were greeted by a swarm of police vehicles. Their place of employment was now a major crime scene.

Denying several requests for a live interview, from different reporters, representing the various area news outlets, Zy'kia dismissed them all with the same statement. "A statement will be released by the department's public relations officer at a later time."

He sat in the driver's seat of his Ford Expedition. The engine on. The cold air hissing through the truck's air conditioning vents was no match for the sweat beads congregating on his forehead. Visions of Gloria, still beautiful in death, were on constant repeat inside his mind.

Zy'kia pondered various scenarios, attempting to understand the whys of Gloria's murder. The action caused him to accept the plain truth. Solving this case would be impossible, without the help of witnesses, or a confession from the killer himself.

***

"While performing his duties, in the early morning hours, an employee of Safe Nights security, discovered the body of thirty-seven-year-old Gloria Walters, in the Santa Rosa Mall's parking lot.

According to family members, Ms. Walters graduated from Fort Walton Beach High. The class of 1987. She'd recently returned to the area after living several years abroad.

Ms. Walters is the seventh victim in a killing spree that has the entirety of Okaloosa County on edge. The police are asking for the public's help. Anyone with information concerning any of the recent murders can call the Fort Walton Police Department, or the Crime Stoppers number located at the bottom left of your television screen."

Transfixed, Javid stared at the television. A tinge of jealousy pricked the hairs of his neck.

She's effin gorgeous! A voice voiced the opinion of all.

"Decorated detective, and former classmate of Ms. Walters, Zy'kia Blunt, refused to make an official statement, but did say, Ms. Walter's murder does not appear to be related to the others. Unquote," the news reporter reported.

"The recent string of murders has left Okaloosa County leaders baffled. There have been more murders committed this month, than the past two years combined," the news reporter continued.

Javid's mind ventured to Poppa. A question he'd asked ricocheted in his head.

"Ever thought of killing someone?"

He didn't take it as more than an inquiry out of curiosity. Now, on further thought, he could hear Poppa's excitement. His tone had an eagerness that prevented his question from being labeled as random.

"Again, the police are asking," the news reporter seeped into Javid's silent assessments.

"Those with information to contact the Fort Walton Beach Police Department or call Crime Stoppers Tip line at 850-242-9671. This is Bryant Durham, reporting live from Okaloosa County on your Channel Three News weekend report."

"In today's other top story," anchorwoman Tonya Gunn picked up the broadcast. "A drive-by shooting on Cypress Street has left a Sylvania Heights man in serious condition. Witnesses say, at approximately 11 pm., a white Chevy Tahoe rode slowly down Cypress Street. Upon making a U-turn, passengers in the vehicle opened fire. This wasn't *a* random shooting, witnesses say, the victim was targeted.

Twenty-two-year-old," using the television's remote control, Javid cut it off.

See, Poppa isn't a wimp, Chip! The voices began.

Did you see how pretty the victim was? Holy moly! A ten on an eight scale!

"Who said, it was Poppa?" Javid whined.

Of course, it was Poppa, Chip. He's not a little whiny crybaby!

"Oh yeah?"

Yeah

"I bet he gets caught. I'm sure he left DNA everywhere."

Stop being a hater, Chip! It isn't a good look.

"Detective Blunt will…"

Is that it? You're afraid of Detective Blunt?

"I'm not afraid of nothing!"

This is us, Chip. Who do you think you're fooling? Then, why didn't you go with Poppa last night?

"Because. Because…" Javid stuttered.

Because you're a wuss! And God, I hate wusses! A voice lent a helping hand.

He's afraid of Zy'kia another interjected.

"No. I was tired," Javid whispered his weak defense, beelining for the bathroom. Bracing himself with both hands on the sink, he stared into the mirror. Its' crack seemed to bisect his face in two halves.

I'm not afraid, he mused inwardly. The thought served to revitalize the voices.

Liar! Liar! Liar! They taunted.

Javid's eyes stretched in their sockets. He fumed, mad at himself for not being able to stand up against the voices.

"Aahhh!" He screamed wildly.

Turning the cold water on full blast, he sheepishly permitted his gaze to return to the mirror. The reflection staring back disgusted him. He plunged his head beneath the freezing stream, praying it'd cleanse him of the voices and his feelings of unworthiness.

***

Florida's bright sun welcomed Poppa as he stepped outside. He inspected his Mazda by eye as he walked to retrieve the day's newspaper.

At a glance, the truck didn't have any damage. The fact tugged a smile onto his features.

His night had gone extremely well. *It was like the heavens gave me their blessings by aligning everything up perfectly for me,* Poppa thought mentally.

Inside, Poppa propped his feet on an unsteady coffee table. He refastened a section of the tape holding his television's remote control together. After multiple attempts, he successfully got the TV to turn on. He tuned into Channel Three News' morning edition, kicked back, and opened the newspaper.

Unsurprisingly, his victim's gaze met his as soon as the paper opened. He scanned through the article half expecting to read his name, or at the very least, see a description of his Mazda.

A breath of relief followed the pronunciation of the article's last word. His name nor truck was mentioned.

He afforded himself another glance at his victim's photo. This time Poppa translated her look to say, *Your secret's safe with me. I took it to the grave.*

Experiencing a gauntlet of emotions opened the door for anxiety to creep in. Poppa's chest tightened. Air filled his lungs in gulps. Anxiety invited its brother, paranoia to the party.

Poppa duck walked to the living room's lone window. Using the thumb and index finger of his right hand, he eased his bedspread curtains aside. He spent the following three and a half minutes peeping outside, before working up the courage to venture out again.

In the fresh air, Poppa swiped at sweat beads holding a rally on his forehead. A breeze blowing off the Gulf of Mexico instigated a family of goosebumps to claim squatter's rights on his left arm.

Ironically, the sun was hot enough to dry out his mouth. It did. His tongue felt heavy, clumsily big, and distorted. He choked down a swallow, while his head pivoted nervously.

A neighbor's infant's cry escaped through an open window. Its wail resembling that of a police cruiser.

Panicking, Poppa managed halting steps, in the direction of his Mazda. From six feet he noticed a splotch of royal blue paint on his front bumper. His heart dropped.

I'm caught He gasped silently while using his right hand to try and erase the paint from his bumper.

Calm down, Poppa. The news reporter didn't mention anything about her car. That means they haven't found it. And they did say, there weren't any witnesses. You're safe. Just calm down and think. Poppa attempted to get a grip.

He leaned on the Mazda's hood. Chest heaving from a series of deep breaths, prescribed to slow his racing heart.

I'll call Javid. He'll know what to do. Poppa's eyes swept up and down the length of his street. A feeling of sickness invaded his entire being. His knees buckled. His worse fears were now a reality.

It's over, He imagined, watching a police cruiser inch its way toward him.

The police car slowly rolled past without the officer paying him the least bit of attention. The weight of the world falling from his shoulders seemed to make Poppa weak. His legs weren't trustworthy. They trembled.

Poppa opened the passenger's door and thankfully collapsed into the front seat. To his dismay, he watched the patrol car stop, reverse, and pull into his driveway.

***

Zy'kia skillfully maneuvered his Ford Expedition through the surge of weekend shoppers on Eglin Parkway. He turned into the K-Mart shopping center's parking lot, using it as a shortcut to the TOPS hamburger joint. While waiting to place his order, he used the time to reminisce on when his love affair with TOPS began. Twenty-one years later, his order remained unchanged.

"Yes. I'd like a double cheeseburger with everything except pickles, and a large tater tot, with an extra-large sweet tea," Zy'kia added a warm smile at the end of his order.

"Coming right up," the drive-thru worker, Pam, returned his smile before sliding the window shut.

Zy'kia used his right knee to steer the Expedition, as he fought to free his double cheeseburger from its grease-stained, wax-paper jail.

After a successful breakout, he took a hearty bite as pay for his efforts. "Better than the first time," He smacked his lips together in pure pleasure.

"Mr. Pride?" Zy'kia addressed a man standing in a driveway.

"Yes? And you are?"

Zy'kia closed his driver's door, wiped a grease spot from his left hand, then answered extending his right.

"Detective Zy'kia Blunt. I'm sorry for your loss," the two men shook hands.

"I understand now not being the best of times, but there are questions that need clearing up. The answers will likely assist in our investigation."

Mr. Pride, Gloria Walter's ex-husband, released Zy'kia's grip. His eyes roamed, expertly sizing up his visitor.

"Sure. Of course, detective. Come in," spinning Mr. Pride led the way inside.

"You'll have to excuse the mess. We've been back in town three days, and most of our things still haven't been unpacked."

"I understand. I've been through it a time or two myself," Zy'kia responded. "It's my knowledge that you and Ms. Walters are divorced?"

"That's true. Please have a seat, detective. We divorced four years ago, but we remained best friends. If you ask me, we became closer after the divorce, than when we were married. But…" Mr. Pride's voice trailed off as he said, "that's neither here nor there now."

Zy'kia spent a split-second wondering what the pain registering on Mr. Pride's features must feel like. Unable to imagine, he concentrated on studying Mr. Pride.

Dark circles highlighted weary eyes. Broad shoulders sagged, causing Mr. Pride to appear constantly slumped and hunched back. His baby afro looked more like a mass conference of naps and tangles.

"Can you provide the names of anyone Ms. Walters hung out with, or considered a friend? It helps immensely if we can determine a timeline of events."

"Last night Gloria went to the Elks Club. She met up with some old girlfriends from her school days for drinks," Mr. Pride's gaze held Zy'kia for ransom.

"I don't understand why anyone would want to hurt her. She was the sweetest..." His voice caught. Struggling to remain composed, Mr. Pride rapidly blinked away tears.

Zy'kia the person sympathized. Zy'kia the detective had a job to perform. "Who were the people she met at the Elks Club?" He asked politely.

Mr. Pride sniffled. He used the back of his right hand to wipe away remnants of his runny nose. "Um. I'm not sure how many there were. I know of two. Leslie Pallace and Carmen Johnstone."

"I need to ask one more question. Then I'll leave you be." Zy'kia paused for a deep breath, then continued, "And how did Ms. Walters get to the Elks Club?"

Mr. Pride's demeanor evolved. Surprise cross-bred with his pain to birth his reaction.

"Wasn't her car found at the scene? She drove."

Zy'kia's expression mirrored Mr. Pride's. His surprise became easily discernable.

She drove?" Zy'kia asked confused.

"A 2008 Royal Blue Acura TL with vanity plates that read: Y U H8 N."

"That news certainly changes things. To answer your question. No, we didn't find her car. We didn't even know a car existed until now.

31

We didn't believe she was killed where her body was discovered. You just confirmed that. Thank you for your time and cooperation, Mr. Pride," Zy'kia rose to his feet.

"I can see myself out," He extended his right hand.

"If there's anything I can assist with, please do not hesitate to call," Zy'kia slipped Mr. Pride his business card.

"Detective?"

"Yes," Zy'kia turned to face Mr. Pride.

"I've heard a lot about you from the television and the papers since we've been back. I'm glad you're on the case. I honestly feel I can depend on you to bring Gloria justice."

CHAPTER 7

"Curt, I need you to find a royal blue 2008 Acura TL. It has personalized license plates that read YUH8N. It belonged to Ms. Walters and is the one thing still missing. I want to know the minute the car is located," Zy'kia pressed end, disconnecting the call.

Backing out of Mr. Pride's driveway, a slight smile creased his features. *He may call me thirty seconds after the car is found. The first twenty-nine will be spent telling Happy.*

Blending with traffic on Beal Parkway, Zy'kia's thoughts ricocheted between Carmen and Leslie. Their names jarred his memory into remembering the bond the three shared in high school. Conjoined triplets were how they were teased.

"Man, I know they are taking this hard," he spoke aloud. Then his mind swerved to reminisce on the relationships he shared with Carmen and Leslie. They were two of his three childhood sweethearts.

Carmen, he'd met in the third grade after moving from Eglin Air Force Base into Fort Walton. She'd been the highlight of his new school, Oakland Heights elementary.

A combination of Black and Puerto Rican, light creamy complexion, wavy, shiny black hair, athletic body, with a supermodel's face. All the ingredients required to convince a ten-year brain that his eyes were beholding the essence of a love recipe.

Another smile. This one is in remembrance of conquering. The chase lasted until their sixth-grade year. A year later, they wouldn't say a word to each other. The silent treatment extended to their senior year of high school.

Zy'kia checked his rearview mirror, slowed to let a late model Buick LA Sabre change lanes, then continued his journey through yesteryear.

Chuckling, he visualized the day he and Carmen decided to cross over imaginary picket lines and break their silence.

With him being the starting point guard for the boys' basketball team at Fort Walton Beach High School, and her for the girls.

While shooting around in the gym weeks before the start of the season. They agreed to a bet on who would average the most points.

"When I win," Carmen flashed all thirty-twos. "You have to take me out to dinner."

"And when you lose?" Zy'kia could hear their voices as if the conversation was currently happening. "What do I get? My mom's gonna feed me, so I don't want no dinner."

"Whatever you want."

"You better be careful with how you say whatever. That could mean anything."

After making a shot, Carmen responded. "Doesn't matter. You're not going to win anyway."

Recalling the day, she gamely paid her debt, Zy'kia's smile stretched to its limits.

He passed over Gap Creek on Beal Parkway with his thoughts swerving to Leslie. Their relationship was the most serious one he'd experienced until Kim.

He met Leslie in his eleventh-grade year. He'd seen her several times while hanging out at Daddy's Money, the local teen club. It wasn't until being introduced by a mutual friend that he spoke to her.

Waiting at the light at the intersection of Mary Esther Cut-off and Beal Parkway, Zy'kia remembered how their initial conversation didn't seem promising. She had a boyfriend.

Less than a month later. I was her boyfriend. Zy'kia bragged within.

The light changed. He made a right onto Mary Esther with his mind hosting him to visions created on the worse day of his life.

They were in Ferry Park Recreation Gym. He, Leslie, and his main man Cedric. Leslie was there as a cheerleader. He and Cedric were there to destroy the competition.

As fate had it. He wouldn't survive the first trip down the court. To this day he refers to Ferry Park as the Tomb because that's where his basketball career died.

Weeks became months that stretched into years with Zy'kia being encrusted in a depressing state of depression. Leslie tried, though she, nor anyone else was able to supply enough love and affection to reattach his broken dream.

The depression instigated experimenting with drugs and alcohol. He found drugs to be unpredictable and too expensive. Yet, the alcohol he could afford, and was great at numbing his pain.

Yep, the alcohol wiped away the pain and Leslie. Zy'kia thought silently.

With his mind steadily cruising down memory lane, Zy'kia failed to spy the royal blue Acura TL parked in the Eglin Federal Credit Union's parking lot.

He traveled on with a foot in the present as well as one in the past. Passing the Santa Rosa Mall, he noticed the massive number of cars.

Most probably don't know there was a body lying on the ground just hours ago.

"Isn't that ironic," Zy'kia spoke aloud to himself. "The one I wanted to love but couldn't. Is now reuniting me with past loves."

***

"Excuse me, sir," the officer slammed his door harder than necessary, then proceeded to approach in Poppa's direction.

Poppa inhaled deeply. Discreetly.

How? So fast? Stay cool. Stay cool. Don't panic. Be cool. Poppa spoke to himself.

"Chyes," Poppa responded, his voice not sounding as strong as he would have liked.

The police officer reached behind his back with his left hand. The action was the undoing of Poppa's last nerve.!

He's reaching for handcuffs His subconscious yelled to his conscious, both wondering why their legs weren't running by now.

Poppa was a heartbeat from pure panic when the officer asked. "Have you seen this cat? It belongs to my mom, and she hasn't been home in a few days and now my mom is worried and now I'm trying to, ah, you know, ah, be a good son and all." The officer's left hand returned, displaying a photocopied copy of a photocopy.

The officer's rambling was heaven-sent. The words were beautiful music, seeing how you're under arrest wasn't in the officer's spiel.

The long wind also provided Poppa time to regain his composure. In doing so, he put on his 'I'm just happy to be in America' face and answered. "No sir. Me no see."

"Dang!" Dejection slumped the officer's shoulders. He pouted.

"Man, I was hoping you could help. All right. Thanks," The officer spun on the ball of his left foot and retreated.

Watching the officer walk away, Poppa basked in the feeling of invincibility. Newly found. Thoroughly enjoyed.

Mental pictures featured his victim, Gloria Walters. Begging. Pleading. Crying. Completely feeling himself, Poppa unclipped his cell phone from his hip. Seconds later, he began speaking.

"Hello, my friend. I was thinking maybe I could come by, and we talk for a while," a brief pause followed in which Poppa wished Javid wouldn't deny his request.

"Sure. I'm not doing much. I'll be here whenever you wanna come," Javid ended the silence.

Wish granted; Poppa smiled.

"Okay, my friend. I come shortly. See you then."

Satisfied, Poppa pulled out of the self-service car wash on the corner of Memorial Drive and Highway 98.

The paint from the Acura washed away, leaving several minor scratches as evidence of the two vehicles colliding. Poppa cruised along Holmes Blvd., feeling the best he'd felt all day. At that moment he decided to ride by the Credit Union to quench his curiosity. His mind worked overtime wondering if the Acura had been located.

Flashing blue lights willed him to the side as a Ford Expedition raced passed. He continued his travels with the Expedition seeming strangely familiar. Turning right onto Jonquil Avenue, his eyes were greeted by a symphony of red and blue lights in the distance.

They found the car, he quickly deduced.

Adrenaline urged him to speed up. Common sense rejected the urge. Poppa continued at the speed limit. His eyes intently surveyed his surroundings.

He arrived at the Credit Union with the light changing from yellow to red. Looking into the Credit Union's parking lot, he noticed yellow crime scene tape stretching diagonally across the far northwest portion.

The Acura's royal blue paint job stood out. A group of uniformed and plain-clothed officers huddled around it.

Swiveling his head to focus on the light, Poppa's eyes momentarily locked with a black plain-clothed officer.

Must be a detective, He unconsciously surmised inwardly.

The light turned green, and Poppa proceeded. On Mary Esther Cut-off he recognized chill bumps peppering his forearms for the first time. He shivered, choosing a right turn onto Lovejoy Road.

"The black man. He looked into my soul," Poppa spoke aloud.

"He knew. It is a... a," Struggling to find the word within his limited vocabulary, Poppa blew his horn at a crackhead prostitute.

Hoping he'd be the supplier for her next fix, she began waving her arms frantically while jumping up and down.

"Premonition!" Poppa shouted his happiness in finding the word. "Premonition," he repeated joyfully.

***

Javid eyeballed Poppa through the peephole for several seconds before answering his knock. The antics being displayed confirmed his assumptions. Poppa was guilty of murder.

He hopped from left leg to right. His eyes were wild, nervously darting inside their sockets.

"Poppa!" Javid greeted as soon as the door swung wide enough to reveal Poppa's figure. "Come in."

Poppa risked a final nervous glance at the streets, then scurried in. Exhaling what one may consider a sigh of relief, Poppa spoke. "Hello, my friend."

Javid studied the mass of raw nerves he called friend.

Jittery as a dope fiend with a cold pipe One of the many voices residing within Javid's skull observed.

Reminds me of a whore that's been asked to attend Sunday services Another supplied its opinion.

"Why are you so nervous?" Javid added a half laugh as a comforter. He stepped around Poppa to reclaim his throne in the form of a thrift store recliner.

"Nervous? Me? No amigo. I'm not nervous." Poppa answered without trying to sit.

"If you say so," Javid allowed. "So," Poppa's peeking through the curtains choked Javid's thoughts. "How many numbers did you get last night?" He finished.

Poppa released the curtain's edge, then fast walked to the front door where he pressed his eye to the peephole.

Labeling this the last straw, Javid asked seriously. "Have you been smoking crack?" His eyes were glued to the back of Poppa's head.

"Huh? Wha...No!" Poppa twirled to face Javid. "Why ask that?"

"Why!" Javid exclaimed with a laugh. "Man, look at you. That's why. Is someone following you or something?"

Poppa helped himself to the bamboo highchair on Javid's left. "I did it," The words were barely audible.

"Hid what?"

"No!" Poppa raised his voice a few octaves. "I said. I did it!" He placed extra emphasis on did.

"Did what?"

Poppa glanced around the room. His eyes once performed a double take. "I did it. Last night."

"Gaalee! You act like that was your first piece of,"

"The murder. Last night," Poppa blurted his interruption.

"I did it!" His eyes rotated to the front door as if he expected the cavalry to come bursting through.

"I pray you were careful not to leave a shred of evidence," Javid spoke assuredly. "Detective Blunt is the best I've ever seen. One slip and it's the big house for you. Remember that."

Poppa rocked back in his chair, then leaned forward. His head bowed to leave his chin resting on his chest. Closing his eyes, he silently admitted.

Exactly what I wanted to hear, my friend.

***

Zy'kia drove east on highway 98 struggling over whom to visit first, Carmen or Leslie. Passing Red Lobster with a decision on the tip of his tongue, his cell phone rang.

"Hello," he answered. "Found the car," Curt's voice provided the welcomed news. "Eglin Federal Credit Union. Corner of Jonquil and Mary Esther."

"On my way! Make sure no one and I mean absolutely no one touches a thing until I get there. Five minutes, tops," Pressing end, Zy'kia activated the Expedition's emergency lights.

He executed a hard right onto Wright Parkway and gave the 310 supercharged horses beneath the hood their head.

Watching the Expedition's speedometer rapidly climb, Zy'kia sorted through the possible routes in search of the fastest.

Discouraged by the amount of traffic on Hollywood Blvd., Zy'kia remained on Memorial Drive.

The four-way stop was thankfully empty as he swerved left onto Holmes Blvd. He sped past Bruner Jr. High and the childhood memories it represented.

Approaching the four-way stop at the intersection of Wright Parkway and Holmes Blvd., Zy'kia switched on the Expedition's sirens to promptly gain the attention of the other drivers. A thousand feet after, he willed the driver of a well-used Mazda pickup to the side of the road.

Magically, the Mazda's operator complied with his wishes. Again, the supercharged horses were free to run.

Three detectives and two patrol units had beaten him to the credit union. "I hope they ain't," Zy'kia cut his thought short. He exited his Expedition to a symphony of flashing police lights.

Curt stood talking with Happy. Two of the three detectives were unspooling yellow crime scene tape marking off the perimeter. The third leaned against the trunk of his Ford Mustang, jotting notes in a notepad.

"There's our baby," Curt sang happily, hitching a finger in the Acura's direction. "No one's been closer than the taped perimeter. Made sure of it myself."

Respecting the yellow tape, Zy'kia made his way to the back of the Acura. Checking the license plate, he read. "Y U H8 N" Turning towards the others, Zy'kia locked eyes with the driver of the Mazda he'd willed aside.

The traffic light turned green, breaking their orbital embrace. Zy'kia followed the Mazda's left onto Mary Esther Cut-off, experiencing the strangest of feelings. He couldn't positively identify the meaning. With his mind running wild as Mexican bulls, he dared not try to connect the Mazda as the source behind his feeling.

CHAPTER 8

Zy'kia lounged on the overstuffed pillows of his tweed sofa. Full as a tick on a fat hound, his mind hummed. After dusting the Acura for DNA evidence, he'd gone to visit Carmen Johnstone.

Initially, he'd fought to suppress his surprise at how she'd allowed herself to decline physically over the years. Five children contributed to her regression.

Wow! Father Time must have some sort of beef with her because he sure hasn't been kind he surmised inwardly.

"Gloria arrived shortly before 11 pm. We had some drinks. Shared some laughs, and all went our separate ways at 1:30 am." He replayed snatches of Carmen's statements.

"No one approached us the entire time. Although she and Leslie were causing a lot of heads to turn. Male and female. But no one approached us."

Zy'kia remembered the time when she'd cause a few double takes herself. Ones that were for the exact opposite reason she'd receive them now.

"We made plans to get together next weekend," Carmen admitted between sobs and shooing her unmannered brood.

"She seemed so full of life, Zy'kia," Her right hand found his left. Pretending to scratch an itch, he immediately removed his hand from its undesirable predicament.

Noticing, but not wanting to accept the fact of another rejection, she continued unfazed.

"Catch whoever is responsible, Zy. Make 'em pay. Gloria deserves justice."

Zy'kia turned his gaze in her direction, "I'll certainly do my best. Right now, we don't have much to work from. To be completely honest. We don't have anything. No suspects. No leads. Nothing! I was hoping you would be able to supply a starting point. Now I'm praying Leslie has something of value," Zy'kia rose from the dinette chair he'd occupied during his visit.

"I believe in you," Carmen stood with him. "I always have."

Zy'kia hugged her, dodged two of her children, and strolled towards the front door. "I'll call Leslie and let her know you'll be stopping by.

The stop at Leslie's went differently. Being closer to Gloria, she was taking her death much harder. Her nine-year-old son, D. Lewis, answered the door. His look crossed curiosity with protectiveness.

"My mom's in there," D. Lewis pointed towards an opened door. "Good luck."

Tentatively, Zy'kia peeped his head inside the room. Leslie lay curled in a ball. Soft sobs expressed her broken heart.

She's still remarkably beautiful Zy'kia observed.

The Caucasian and Pilipino blood in her veins combined to give her skin the appearance of a yearly tan. Her round face housed large, brown, doe-like eyes. Her hair was cut short, she resembled Demi Moore in the movie Ghost.

Unlike Carmen, Leslie stayed in shape after bearing children. He felt directly related to the pain she attempted to release through tears. The burning in his soul confirmed what he'd debated over the years since they decided separation was best. He remained in love.

"Hey Gyps," Zy'kia used the nickname he'd given her many years prior. "You okay?" He asked, fighting the urge to wrap his arms around her.

She responded by shaking her head in the negative, but she did provide a weak smile.

"Perhaps I should return another time," Zy'kia suggested.

"No," The forcefulness of her tone aborted Zy'kia's retreat. "You two go play in your rooms, while I talk with Detective Blunt," surprisingly her children listened without rebuttal.

"Nice kids," Zy'kia complimented.

"Until they get used to you and then the real them surfaces," A torn laugh joined the weak smile.

Carmen could surely use a few sessions in your parenting 101 class Zy'kia admitted.

"Please sit," Leslie fanned her right hand in the direction of a loveseat opposite her position on the couch.

"Thanks. Carmen has pretty much told me how y'all's night began and ended. I hate to make you relive this, but I need to hear your version, in case she inadvertently missed something of importance," Zy'kia lowered his six-foot frame into the loveseat.

She sat up, found a stronger smile to present, then began her story. At completion, she'd confirmed all that Carmen had said. Her testimony didn't include the golden ticket to the apprehension and conviction of Gloria's killer. However, it did reignite feelings he'd believed to have been defused years ago.

Blindsiding him, Leslie steered their conversation in an unexpected direction. "I've been keeping up with you from a distance. Shoot, it'd be hard not to, seeing how you're in the papers and on the news so often. Still our hero," she rolled to place her feet on the Mohawk Wear-Dated Collection carpet.

Get you something to drink?" she questioned standing. "We have Kool-Aid," the accompanying smile was big and genuine.

"Well since you're using my weakness against me," They shared a laugh. "Suppose I will take a glass of Kool-Aid," Zy'kia held her eyes with his.

"And since you mentioned it. The bigger the glass the better," He watched the sway of her hips through the thin fabric of her pajamas.

"I can't believe you remembered how much I like Kool-Aid," Zy'kia reached for the glass in her left hand.

"Remember? There's no way I'll ever forget. Not with all the Kool-Aid, I've made to quench your thirst," Leslie returned.

Lowering his glass, Zy'kia smacked his lips. "This," He hefted the glass in a faux salute. "Reminds me of the fact that I've been missing the way you combine artificial flavors with the appropriate amount of sugar. Now, this is what you call Kooool-Aiiiid!"

Another laugh.

"Do you believe E is involved in some way? If so, I wouldn't be able to live with myself. I convinced her to divorce him." She swallowed a mouthful of Kool-Aid. "Too much sugar," she said positively.

"Too much? I was leaning toward maybe needing like um... a pin head more. I only met E today. Judging by the vibe I got from him, I'd say no. But it doesn't mean much. As of now, anyone could be her killer. Therefore, everyone has to be vetted."

"Since laying here thinking, I realized I suggested she leave E because I didn't have the nerve to leave Ron." Zy'kia peered over the top of his glass to find Leslie staring at him intently.

"My life is so freakin' miserable! I swear! I put on my happy face for the children's sake. Truthfully, Ron would hardly notice if I packed up and left today." The depth of her revelation enticed Zy'kia to take two giant gulps.

Recognizing his uncertainty, Leslie added, "Probably shouldn't be telling you this huh? It's just that Gloria's death has made me realize...life is too short. For years, I have wanted to reach out to you. Why?" Her tone softened. Her eyes engaged his.

"To be my knight in shining armor. I know it sounds silly and immature, but I wished you'd rescue me. Whisk me away to forever after," Leslie lowered her head, relinquishing eye contact she continued.

"I heard about you marrying Kim, and I refused to disrespect her. Y'all's marriage. I didn't think it was right to interfere with your marriage because mine was a bad joke.

Then the papers advertised y'all's divorce and even tried to scandalize your name. I wanted to be there for you, but my being married forced me to stay in my place. Only today do I realize, this isn't my place. I'm not happy. I can't pretend anymore. I'll lose my mind."

Leslie's shocking confessions dried up Zy'kia's mouth like the Mojave Desert in mid-August at high noon. He reached for his Kool-Aid.

"Hard to believe?" His reaction inspired her question. "It shouldn't be, considering our history. Still, at times I find it kind of absurd myself. But…" She placed her right hand over her heart. "It's the truth. The whole truth, and nothing but the truth. So, help me, God!"

Feeling the need to rid herself of the excess weight, Leslie went on. "Think of how close we were. Then, think of how we ended. You can't tell me that you haven't beaten yourself with what if this and what if that," She bunched her eyebrows.

"You were my first love, Zy'kia. My everything. Sure, we were merely teenagers. Truth is," Leslie stabbed a freshly manicured finger in her heart. "You've never left here! I had to move on with my life. You didn't leave much of a choice. I simply moved on with my mind and body. My soul remained with its mate." A fresh torrent of tears cascaded down her cheeks.

"I'm leaving Ron. I may never regain the missing piece to my puzzle, but at least I can stop pretending to be something and someone I'm not." Zy'kia gulped down the remainder of his Kool-Aid.

Laughing, Leslie exclaimed. "Calm down! I'm not trying to lasso you. I just wanted the words off my chest and in the open before it became too late to say them. Plus, I made a promise to Gloria that I'd tell you how I felt. She's the only one I've shared this with over the years. I love you, Zy'kia."

Several silent seconds ticked away with them both digesting the preceding words. Ending the silence, Zy'kia cleared his throat.

"Since we're confessing," He nervously fiddled with his empty glass. "You're the reason me and Kim didn't work."

"Me?" Leslie wondered.

"You." Zy'kia agreed.

"What I'm trying to say is, I understand exactly what you mean. I feel and have felt the same way for all these years." Gazing deep into the windows of Leslie's soul, Zy'kia added. "I could give Kim everything, but my heart."

Another long breath passed before Zy'kia pushed to his feet. "Gyps, I'm glad we're having this discussion. Even wished it would have happened years sooner. The problem is this isn't the proper place to be having it. I don't know Ron, but I won't let that make me disrespect his house.

Joining him on her feet, Leslie assured. "I understand. You were always the good guy," She included a smile as she led the way to the front door.

Opening the door, she asked. "Can we finish this another time?"

Zy'kia stepped across the threshold answering, "Would love to!"

"Give me a few days and I'll call you."

"And I'll answer three rings tops."

"Three?" Leslie feigned dejection. "What happened to two?"

"Time," Zy'kia stated simply.

"I'm not as fast as I once was." He stepped up into the Expedition's cab. His left arm snaked out of the driver's window. The pinky, index, and thumb raised in what the unknowing might consider a gang sign.

He pushed his arm forward in a swooping motion. From the doorway, Leslie parroted the act. It was a gesture they'd always used when departing each other's company. Sign language for I love you.

CHAPTER 9

Poppas lounged at the exact table he claimed the night before. Again, he chose 1800 Silver Tequila as his choice of poison. He swirled the ice in the glass desperately trying to figure out what caused Javid to act as he had.

At first, he blamed Javid for being jealous. Perhaps even upset for his not including him. As time passed with him sitting in Javid's apartment, he'd come to realize. Javid was far from being jealous. "Whatever his problem is. Thank God it's his and not mine." That declaration ushered in more pleasant thoughts.

Poppa's thought process gravitated back to the night before. "Gloria," she'd said her name was. Her voice was timid, trembling with fright. Remembering the wild-eyed glare, she'd greeted him with upon regaining consciousness, Poppa swallowed down an unhealthy inhale of Tequila.

"Relax and be cool," He'd informed her. "That is if you wish to remain alive."

Once inside his apartment, Poppa inquired, "Are you afraid, Gloria?" Without hesitation, her head bobbed the obvious answer.

"I don't understand why you are doing this to me."

Ignoring her, Poppa allowed his eyes to molest the contour of her body. His last sexual encounter was long past remembrance. Although the aching in his loins voted to end the drought, Poppa realized to do so would realistically end his criminal career. As well as his life.

"Do you want to live, Gloria?" Her head bobbed her reply.

"Do as I say, and you won't have any problems at all. I'm going to free your arms and legs, but if you scream or attempt to flee. I promise on Sweet Mother Mary. I will kill you." Using a humongous butcher knife, Poppa removed the tape from her ankles and wrists.

With her gaze fixated on the scary knife, Gloria's fear was etched deeply into her facial features. "Are you the guy that's been killing all those people?"

Briefly, Poppa entertained the thought of lying. Deciding against it, he answered honestly. "No. I am not. Furthermore, I've never killed anyone. And I pray you are not my first," He lied.

"Are you going to rape me?" A smidgen of relief intermingled with her fear.

Poppa rubbed across the hardness in his lower region. The thought alone was pleasing. But the potential side effects were enough to resist temptation. He understood to leave his DNA would be equivalent to committing suicide.

His delay in answering her question induced Gloria to draw conclusions. "Okay. I won't resist. Please, don't kill me. I'm afraid to die."

Tears parachuted from her eyelids. A portion crashed into various regions of her face. While the others splashed down onto imitation hardwood flooring.

Reluctantly, Poppa offered Gloria a moment of clarity. "No Gloria. I'm not going to rape you," he said without a hint of enthusiasm.

"Well, is it money you want? I don't have.."

"I don't want money," he silenced her. "Presently, I'm unsure how to explain the reason you're here."

Overrun by confusion, her fears began to ebb. "Let's just say, you're here for my pleasure. A short time for me to look at you. Bask in your beauty so to speak."

The tears resumed. "Please Gloria. Your tears are spoiling the mood for me. Perhaps you'd like a drink. Forgive me, but all I have to offer is Tequila." Gloria used the palm of her right hand to wipe at the tears. They continued falling.

"Have you forgotten our agreement so soon?" Poppa asked. "Failure to comply with my wishes…" He permitted the remainder of his statement to linger. It was sufficient for Gloria to receive his message. She immediately focused her attention on getting herself under control.

Confident she wouldn't attempt any foolishness, Poppa disappeared into the kitchen. Several sniffles escorted him back into the living room. Her crying stopped; Gloria looked frightened as a gazelle in a lion's den.

Clutching her knees to her chest, Gloria rocked back and forth. "Why me?" Her inquiry was a mere whisper.

Poppa placed two glasses on a milk crate coffee table within her reach. Both contained three ice cubes. Pouring alcohol into the glass nearest her, he provided an answer.

"Because my dear Gloria. You were the fairest of them all." Poppa nudged the glass of Tequila in her direction. Saluting with his glass, he added, "To us." Then emptied his glass like a true professional.

He smacked his lips as the Tequila burned its way to his stomach. "Aren't you going to join me in a drink?"

Fearful of the consequences of not complying, she hefted her glass to her lips. "Now you say it. Say, to us, Gloria."

"To us," she muttered weakly then half-heartedly sipped the fiery liquid.

***

Entranced by re-runs of The Andy Griffith Show, Javid laughed as Deputy Barney Fife escorted Otis, the town's drunk, into his personal jail cell.

He'd spent much of his afternoon embroiled in heated discussions with the voices. They disagreed over Poppa's trustworthiness.

The voices wanted to include Poppa in their extra-curricular activities. He didn't feel Poppa was capable of outsmarting

Detective Blunt. Committing the murder was the easy part. Staying free was the task.

"Running comes naturally to the fox, outwitting the hound is what he must learn to do," he'd told Poppa.

Feeling the voices starting to warm up, Javid hurriedly directed his attention towards the television. All to no avail.

Chip! The voices called. *After all we've been through? You need us, Chip.*

Javid engrossed himself deeper into Barney's antics as he pleaded with Andy to allow him to load his gun with his one bullet to help apprehend a gang of bank robbers.

Chip, you can't ignore us. You. Us. We're all the same. Friends till the end.

Giving in to his tormentors, Javid cried out. "I've made up my mind. I'm not changing it!"

Just hear us out, Chip. Reason with us.

Yeah, compromise why don'tcha? Another voice added.

"Leave me alone!" Javid whined. "I'm watching Andy and Barney."

Forget Andy and Barney! What has either of them ever done for you? Where were they when the doctors were sticking you with needles? Filling your body with only God knows what. I'll tell you where they were. They were tucked away in cozy freakin' Mayberry, Chip. That's where they were. And where were we? By your side. We are the ones that held you down.

Realizing there wouldn't be any peace until he listened to what the voices had to say, Javid leaned forward and lowered the television's volume. "Okay, I'll hear you out. But that doesn't mean I'll cooperate with your plan, especially if it involves Poppa in any way." Leaning back, Javid closed his eyes, giving the voices complete access to his mind.

Can't you tell, Chip? We're on the verge of being famous. The entire county is terrified! A few more victims and they'll create a series called 'C.S.I. Okaloosa'.

A master in the art of manipulation, the voice pressed on. *You should contact the detective. What's his name? Yeah, Zy'kia Blunt. The Hound Dog.*

Well, I think you should show him that we're slicker than any other fox he's chased. Let's play a deadly game with him. We'll call it Fox Hunt. The rules will be simple. The longer it takes for the hound to catch the fox. The more people die.

Oooh! That sounds like a cool game. I wanna play!

Me too!

Yeah, me too!

The voices all began to clamor. Each one voiced their desire to participate in the game.

Javid shook his head violently to get the voices to settle down. Soon the voice of his conscience regained the microphone.

I know you don't want to include Poppa but hear me out. We'll use Poppa as a pawn. He'll keep The Hound Dog sniffing the wrong scent. Sound like a plan, Chip?

"So y'all consider killing innocent people just a game?"

Sure Chip. And it's better than drawing friggin circles around the pictures that don't belong.

"What about Poppa? I can't sacrifice my friend."

Sure, you can! And you will. If you want to keep our ass out of the electric chair. You saw Poppa. The blood on his hands has him out of control. It's the power bug. Plus, the fact that he's your friend would make it even more special for him, knowing he was able to protect his friend. I'm sure he'd think you'd do the same for him. Trust me, Chip. Have I ever led you astray?

***

"Thanks," Poppa added a smile for the waitress who'd delivered his fresh glass of 1800 Silver Tequila. Watching her pocket his two-dollar tip, he admired the sway of her hips as she scurried to the next customer.

Poppa reclined in his chair, tilted his head to a comfortable angle, closed his eyes, and continued reflecting on the biggest night of his life.

"This is the point where you get undressed," Poppa's tone hinted at what would happen if she failed to comply.

Slowly, Gloria rose to her feet. "I'm not talking about simply taking your clothes off. I want you to take them off seductively. I want you to make me feel like I'm wanted. Can you do that for me, Gloria?"

Silent tears streamed. Afraid to look her problems in the eyes, Gloria's head drooped as she said, "I thought you said, you weren't going to rape me."

"I'm not. Just like I'm not gonna kill you. Unless you make me."

Deciphering the statement's underlying meaning, Gloria loosened the top button of her blouse. Her hips gyrated, grinding the air as if it were the world's greatest lover. Risking a glance in Poppa's direction, she inhaled sharply.

He stood caressing the largest piece of manhood she'd ever seen. He stroked it to the rhythm of her movements.

"Come closer, Gloria. Don't be afraid."

Afraid? That was hours ago. She mused inwardly. I'm bout to leave the terrified classification any minute now. Okay, get a grip. Gloria prodded herself.

You're strong enough to overcome anything that may happen. Do not make him kill you. Understand? Do not make him kill you!

In that instance, she decided to survive this ordeal, pick up the pieces, and move forward with her life. Survival instincts placed her right foot in front of her left. She shuffled towards Poppa not knowing she'd received a death sentence the moment she walked into the Elks club.

Unbelievably, Gloria began dancing with a newfound zeal. Her hips snapped back, front, and side to side, in tune with an imaginary beat.

"Touch it." Poppa extended his penis in her direction.

Squeezing her eyes shut tight, Gloria reached out until her hand brushed against his. She thought of pleasant memories, as her hand slid across Poppa's wrist onto the pulsating shaft.

"Stroke it," Poppa suggested.

She obeyed. Gloria massaged Poppa's penis with practiced skill. Pleasure closed his eyes. The act seemingly caused hers to open. The large butcher knife immediately came into view.

Grab it! Her mind screamed. Now! Got Dammit! Grab the knife. The knife!

Finally breaking through the fog shrouding her mind, Gloria's left hand began the slow descent toward the butcher knife.

Poppa's eyes fluttered open. The disturbance in the rhythm she'd set to blame. He instantly noticed her left arm suspended in air. His eyes continued on, to spy the butcher knife inches from the tips of her fingers, making her arm's destination obvious. The guilty look marring her features supplied the necessary two to make four.

Infuriated, Poppa hissed in Spanish, "Tu' Puta!" He backhanded her, splitting both lips.

Gloria reeled from the blow. Its pain quickly dissipated. The crazed look etched into Poppa's face frightened it away. She realized she'd made a costly mistake. And the price would likely be her life.

Revulsion fueled Poppa's charge from the chair he'd commandeered. Oddly, Gloria's mind strayed to cover her nakedness. Closing her eyes, she braced herself for the blows she was certain to come. Yet, none came.

Curiosity opened her left eye to a slit. A shadow trekked across her peripheral a heartbeat before she felt a rough nylon texture wrap around her neck. Another heartbeat left her gasping for breath. Her hands flew up to her neck, wrestling with the apparatus depriving her of air.

No luck.

Slipping into the bright rays of light, Gloria thought of friends and family. She wanted to relay her dreams and aspirations. Inform him that she wished to become a mother and grandmother. The hot breath simmering her neck decreased the likelihood of any of these things manifesting.

The bright rays dimmed. The light highlighted a tunnel. She drifted towards it. Cautiously navigating her way through the darkness. Her child self-reached out to escort her into the tunnel's entrance. Gladly, Gloria accepted the hand. Her fighting was over.

Poppa peered over the rim of his glass, as his left hand directed his drink towards his mouth. No one paid him the least bit of attention.

He shivered, remembering the gentleness of Gloria's touch. Luckily, he'd opened his eyes in time to negate her wicked intentions. The ensuing rage was overwhelming. He reacted and was surprised by the reaction.

Dominance.

Powered by the sensation, Poppa dug deeper into its essence. He squeezed. Harder. And still harder. Reality returned with him drenched in sweat. Gloria's corpse lay draped across the arm of his worn couch. A wet, stickiness lured Poppa's gaze to his right hand. He'd killed two lives by snuffing out one.

CHAPTER 10

Happy for the reprieve in the murders, Zy'kia jousted with a degree of frustration over the slow progress in solving the cases. The perpetrator was extra careful to not leave a shred of evidence. It'd been three weeks since Gloria's death, and they weren't a step closer to learning the killer's identity.

Several calls had been made to the tip line, but the information left was about as helpful as a raincoat would be to a dolphin.

Carmen called a few times pretending to be concerned about the investigation. She quickly guided their conversation to a personal level. At this time, Zy'kia hurriedly discovered an excuse to end the call.

Carmen didn't bother trying to disguise her interest in him. She'd made it clear of his being welcomed at her home. She went as far as to provide her husband's work schedule. Visions of her five children depleted any chance of him taking her up on her offer.

He hadn't spoken with Leslie since the day he left her house. She'd left a message on his answering machine relaying the fact that she'd asked Ron, her husband, for a divorce.

He'd considered returning her call, disguising his true intentions with the investigation.

Zy'kia recalled the difficult moments he'd withstood during his divorce. Hers included children, complicating matters even worse.

Being alone in his office, Zy'kia spoke aloud as he usually did. "Coulda picked a better time, Gyps." He shot a Nerf basketball at a hoop hanging on the back of his office's door.

Brick.

"Detective Blunt," Zy'kia answered the phone on his desk.

Silence.

"Detective Blunt," He repeated.

More silence.

The guys in the precinct often played practical jokes in this fashion. He held the phone anticipating the heavy breathing he was sure to come next. A low whisper sounded in his ear instead.

"Know why I didn't stop after the first victim?" Zy'kia's body sprang forward. "Because Detective, killing is like eating a Lays potato chip. You can't stop with just one."

"What victim are you referring to?" Zy'kia pressed.

Silence.

"Is this your version of a prank, Curt?"

Silence.

"Come on. Talk to me. Isn't that why you called."

"I called to determine if you're as smart as everyone makes you out to be. Seventy-two percent rate of solving cases? Some may think that to be impressive, Detective."

Zy'kia analyzed the voice. He quickly deemed the heavy syrupy southern accent to be fake.

"Hell. I'm not the least bit impressed. The individuals you compiled those stats against weren't worthy to be called criminals. They're as bogus as your fictional seventy-two percent," the caller interrupted. His taunting laughter infuriated Zy'kia.

"Zy'kia. You don't mind if I call you Zy'kia, do you?"

"No. I don't. Since we're on a first-name basis. What should I call you?"

More laughter.

"That'll be clear by the time I hang up. Have you noticed how terrified the good citizens of Okaloosa County are? They leave their homes and pray they'll make it back to them. Why?

Because they don't have faith in your seventy-two percent either. They don't trust you. It's apparent the oath you swore, and the shield you wear is fraudulent." Rage rippled through Zy'kia. He held the phone receiver with a death grip.

"You can tell me about the percentage when I'm putting the cuffs on you. See how.."

"Now. Now. Detective," the caller laughed. "Just how do you plan on doing that? You are not qualified, Zy'kia. But you are now involved in a game they didn't prepare you for in the academy. Like it or not. Innocent lives are depending on you. Your failure will be the direct result of someone's death. How does that make you feel?"

The laughter ended as abruptly as it started. "Starting this very minute. You're on a fox hunt. You're the hound, and now you know what you should call me." The phone line went dead in Zy'kia's ear. He slammed the phone into the cradle with so much force. The receiver cracked.

***

Cruising, on the prowl for a fresh kill, Poppa steered his Mazda pickup off Racetrack Road and made a right turn onto Denton Boulevard. He'd been feasting on the exuberant feeling of raw power. A sensation acquired with his first kill.

Today, the feeling no longer existed, although its' addictive powers insisted, that he does whatever is `necessary to regenerate the high.

At the intersection of Denton Boulevard and Bob Sikes Boulevard, Poppa hardly noticed the two crack stars smiling at him as he braked for the four-way stop. It'd require more than junky prostitutes dying slow deaths to satisfy his thirst for blood. He sought those who cherished their lives.

"I'll do whatever you want. Please, don't kill me," Gloria's voice rang inside his head as a reminder.

Turning left onto Mayflower Avenue, Poppa decided to refine his search to a more upscale neighborhood.

***

Zy'kia sat at his desk fuming. The killer's cockiness to blame. It was bad enough to not be making any headway as far as solving the murders goes. But to have the killer call and mock him sent things to another level.

He was certain it was the killer on the opposite line. The reference to the potato chips insured that. The potato chip bags found at the crime scenes were deliberately kept from the media. To mention them meant the person speaking had to be the killer, or at least someone close to the killer. Either way, it was a person Zy'kia wanted to talk to.

This is a game to him. A fox hunt. Okay, buddy. I'm on your trail. He declared inwardly.

People are dying. This is far from a game. What if I can't catch him? Doubt began to creep into Zy'kia's thought process.

How many innocent lives is he willing to take? The phone ringing on his desk startled Zy'kia back to the present.

He stared at the phone as it rang for the third time. His right hand hovered over the receiver. *Is he calling back?* he wondered.

Snatching the phone from its cradle at the beginning of the fifth ring, Zy'kia held the phone to his ear without speaking. He expected to hear the sinister low whisper of the killer's voice. Receiving neither, he said. "Detective Blunt."

"Does it always take that long for you to answer your phone? Or am I disturbing you?" The sound of Leslie's angelic voice washed away Zy'kia's mounting anxiety.

"Gyps?" he asked stupidly.

"How many other chics are calling you?" There wasn't a hint of playfulness in her tone.

"Oh. It's you," Zy'kia dug himself in deeper.

"Oh. It's you? What exactly is that supposed to mean? I'll hang up so whoever you wished it to be can get through."

"Gyps. Wait. That's not how I meant it. I. I"

59

"Yes? Go ahead," Leslie interjected.

"I…"

"What I thought. Anyways?" Leslie refused to allow him to remove any of the dirt rapidly filling his hole.

"Gyps, it's been a.."

"Save the lies, Zy'kia. I didn't call for them. Plus, you're still not good at it," anger dominated Leslie's tone.

"I'm calling to invite you to dinner. I was thinking we could finish our conversation, but now I believe I'd rather eat alone."

"Please, Gyps. Don't do that," Zy'kia spoke firmly. "I'd love dinner, and to finish our conversation. I've had my share of late nights surfing through what-ifs. When and where?"

"My, putting your foot down always did turn me on," Leslie's smile was visible through the phone line.

"You just don't know how my day has been," Zy'kia paused to upload the proper words. Leslie beat him to the punch.

"You can inform her that she officially has competition."

Laughing, Zy'kia responded, "If you only knew. I'm single. I'm not seeing anyone. I'm not sleeping with anyone. It's been this way since my divorce."

Eight seconds of awkward silence elapsed before Leslie chose to say, "Forgive me, Zy. I'm a little stressed myself. Dinner's at 7:30. The where is, 1823-Pointed Leaf Lane. A townhouse in Greenacres. Think you can find it?"

"Gyps, I'm a detective. I specialize in finding things."

"Oh yeah. I almost forgot about your seventy-two percent rate of solving cases." She smiled. He frowned.

***

Javid lingered next to the pay phone outside of Publix in Sun Plaza Shopping Center. A full-fledged smile bisected the lower portion of his face. He envisioned Detective Blunt throwing a hissy fit inside his office, swearing to the heavens that he'd catch the fox if it was the last thing he ever did.

Walking into Publix, Javid's thoughts migrated to Poppa. A jealous tick revealed itself. Poppa's one kill garnered nearly as much media attention as all his combined.

He's trying to steal your glory, Chip. The voices instigated.

Did you see how pretty she was?

A beauty queen for Poppa. Beauty nor queen for us!

Maybe we rollin' inside the wrong head

Javid looked away from the bunch of bananas under his inspection, to find an old lady staring directly at him.

"How are you today, young man?" she asked.

"Fine, and you?" Javid returned.

Big bad Chip doesn't even scare old ladies! What a wuss! The voices continued.

"I'm making it. Getting my shopping in before dark," she dropped a bag of oranges into her cart as proof. "I wouldn't dare leave my house after dark with that crazed lunatic on the loose." Her choice of words caused Javid to cringe. "Did you see the pretty Lil gal he killed last week? She was the most precious thang you ever did see."

The old windbag didn't even mention one of your victims, Chip. Poppa's stealing your shine homeboy. The voices taunted as he added mangoes and bananas to the shopping cart.

Yeah. We rollin' inside the wrong head!

Javid relaxed within his cozy one-bedroom duplex on Bobolink Street. He chose to live modestly, although he could easily afford life's finer things. Being the only child, of an only child. He inherited the fortune his grandparents accumulated during their lifetimes.

He shoveled his spoon into a bowl of Breyers Mint Chocolate Chip ice cream. This was his idea of splurging.

"Leave the child alone. He simply has a chip on his shoulder," he recalled his grandmother defending another one of his misdeeds. That was the origination of his nickname, Chip.

Good ol' Grams, he thought silently. *I miss you, Grammy. You're the one person that ever understood me. Consequently, you're the only one I ever cared for.*

He smiled, visualizing his grandmother raising hell after hearing the news of his mother agreeing to send him to Chattahoochee.

Feeling sorry for yourself, Chip?

Perhaps a little down? Another voice added.

I can't believe you're in here acting like a baby. Boohoo I miss my Grammy. Another voice was less compassionate.

Poppa's out becoming famous, and we're stuck inside. Really?

Really. Another seconded. *Told y'all we're rollin' inside the wrong head!*

Chip, it's time to make us world-renowned. Tonight, we're giving the hound reasons to pick up the pace. Unless, of course, you're too crazy to be a sly fox?

Javid reacted according to the voice's plan. He flung his unfinished bowl of ice cream across the room. It smacked into the wall. The bowl and spoon clamored to the floor, leaving a glob of Mint Chocolate Chip trailing down wood grain wallpaper in its wake.

"Don't call me crazy!" he yelled.

"Don't you ever call me crazy!" he became more furious.

"You want crazy? I'll show you crazy!" he kicked his thrift store coffee table, splintering the poster board in the process.

"How's that for crazy? Huh?"

"I'll show the world crazy! Tonight! Do you hear me? Tonight!"

CHAPTER 11

Picking her up proved to be easier than Poppa imagined. It was simple as pulling into Pirate's Cove liquor store, to buy a bottle of Jose Cuervo, and there she was walking through the parking lot.

Poppa followed her naturally blonde hair until the vision transformed into large breasts, probably the result of implants, that stretched the fabric of her halter top.

He trailed downward still. Sky blue daisy duke shorts scarcely covered the v of her crouch, and that would later be credited as the beginning to her end.

Forcefully, Poppa willed his eyes upward. Curious to see if her face complimented the entirety of her assets.

Wow! He exclaimed inwardly, as he whipped his Mazda into a parking space. In that instance, her sea-green eyes met his hazel.

"Beautiful," he admitted.

Opening his door, he was greeted with, "What does a damsel in distress have to do to get a lift?"

"No more than waiting for her knight in shining armor to return from inside the store. It's unlocked," he motioned towards his truck. "Sit down. Make yourself comfy. I'll be back in a flash."

"Didn't know if you drink, but I brought you a cup anyways," Poppa extended an ice-filled cup, as he climbed into the cab. The bottle followed. "It's Tequila. Jose," he said.

She accepted the proffered goods. "I'm not choosy about what I drink, or whom I drink it with. Long as the shots get poured."

Chuckling, Poppa responded, "Where ya headed?"

"With this unopened bottle in my lap, it's nearly impossible for me not to be headed in your direction." She'd never get a chance to make another bad decision.

***

Zy'kia nervously stood outside Leslie's door holding a fresh bouquet of Lilies in his left hand. Her favorite flower. His right hand contained a fifth of Pinot Grigio red wine. To go along with their pasta and red sauce dinner.

Inhaling deeply, he exhaled the remaining particles of nervousness, then pressed the doorbell. Within four eye blinks, Leslie opened her front door.

She wore a purple body dress that ended slightly above her knees. Its rayon material accentuated her every curve. She smiled as Zy'kia goggled.

"You like?" she asked performing a full turn.

Zy'kia scrutinized the masterpiece in front of him. "Marvelous. Simply marvelous," he held out the bouquet of Lilies. "Beauty for a beauty."

"I won't have any furniture for a few more days," Leslie informed him as she led them into her home's interior.

They sat at a lawn table. In lawn chairs. In the middle of the townhouse's spacious dining room. Empty plates with remnants of the pasta and red sauce dinner they'd enjoyed accompanied the wine glasses they now sipped from on the table's top.

Huckleberry Sugar Blossom scented candles served as the room's fragrance and light. The sounds of Luther Vandross' soulful voice provided solace during private thoughts.

"So," Leslie began sipping from her glass. "You've missed me over the years huh?"

Gazing deep into her dark browns, Zy'kia replied suavely. "That's an understatement."

She blushed.

Stevie Wonder could see the chemistry that drew them together initially. Throughout dinner, they'd filled the other in on the events that had transpired in their individual lives.

Sixteen long years had passed since their separation. Yet, their bond remained intact.

Reaching across the table, Leslie placed her right hand over his left. "Do you think there's a future for us?"

Zy'kia paused. Not to search for an answer, but to stealthily add dramatic effect. "Honestly Gyps," he looked away.

More theatrics.

"I haven't thought that far ahead. Right now, this itself is so unbelievable. That we're here, together, even having this conversation. I don't want to ruin the feeling by overthinking. For the time being, I rather just enjoy your presence and cherish every moment we spend. Time will reveal our future. Together, or not. I will always love you."

Leslie tried unsuccessfully to blink away the lone tear pooling in her left eye. It spilled over her eyelid and began its descent down her left cheek.

***

"Why is my father being the sheriff of Okaloosa County so hard to believe?" The bottle of Jose rested on a worn milk crate coffee table, half empty, or half full, depending on the perspective of the eyes looking at it.

"That's not what I find hard to believe," Poppa replied, taking a toke on the joint he held in his right hand. "It's that his daughter is partying in my apartment. That's what's hard to believe."

Inwardly, he followed with. *The entire county is gonna be shaken up when they discover your body.* He gazed straight into her eyes.

Angelique Norris, daughter of Okaloosa county sheriff, Carlton Norris found strangled. Poppa envisioned the headlines her murder was sure to create.

"You're not having fun. I want you to have fun!" Angelique pouted. "I'm boring you. I'll go." She stood to leave.

"No sweetheart," Poppa pulled her down beside him on his sofa that was almost as old as her. "That's not what I want. I'm having a ball and the real fun hasn't even begun."

"Oh, it hasn't?" She asked flirtatiously accepting the joint from Poppa.

***

Javid sat on an enormous beach towel in the shadows cast by the two dunes flanking him. A quarter past 10 pm. The pedestrian traffic walking the beach had slowed to a trickle.

Be patient Chip. We want a pretty one.

Yeah. Prettier than Poppa's!

He watched the lights of the beach patrol's four-wheeler fade into the distance. A strong breeze blew off the Gulf of Mexico, bringing with it the scent of salt.

The rush of waves ending their journey by crashing onto the shore, blended with the shrill cry of seagulls searching for a late snack. The cloud of death exuding from Javid's physical contradicted the otherwise serene setting.

The words of Karen White's song Superwoman drifted on the breeze. Javid froze, listening, attempting to pinpoint the direction. His eyes scanned the darkness. Nothing. He refocused on the expanse of dunes surrounding him. The same result. Nothing.

Strangely, the female's voice grew nearer. Her words were clearer. Yet, her presence hadn't materialized out of the darkness.

Javid crouched. Blending in with beach shrubbery, he swept his eyes in a half-moon to his left. Repeating the act to his right, Javid tensed. A motion began to take shape as a shadowy figure approached, singing..

Adrenaline swooshed into every corridor of Javid's body. His heart rate increased, though his breathing remained calm.

His eyes locked in. Mentally, he began to detach from reality. He morphed to another time. In another world. Where he was the savior, tasked with the duty of ridding society of its undesirables.

The moon peeked from behind a mass of clouds. Its light captured a female strolling between two dunes, putting them on a collision course.

Close enough for Javid to distinguish her body's curves, he could also hear the pain in her voice as she continued to sing.

From twenty feet Javid was certain she'd walk right over him. Five feet astonished Javid. She was far prettier than Poppa's kill, making her the perfect victim.

Excited, the voices began to rumble. Javid shook his head violently to quiet them.

No luck.

She's the one Chip!

America's Most Wanted! Here we come, baby!

On she came. Two feet. Javid braced himself for the inevitable. One foot came amid a high note.

The showstopper.

The crescendo found her toppling over him. A light shriek was followed by an audible gush of wind, as she landed flatly on Javid's beach towel.

Her head lolled, introducing her eyes to Javid's. An embarrassed chuckle parted her lips. "My bad," she said. "I had my eyes closed. I mean, I wasn't expecting anyone to be...Well um...you know," she pushed to her knees.

Without a word of warning, Javid plunged a syringe into the female's upper chest. She grabbed at his hands far too late. The heartache she'd experienced moments earlier didn't feel nearly as bad as the ache paining her heart now.

She clutched her chest. Wide-eyed. Her gaze pinpointed Javid, but her eyes refused to see. Bright lights dimmed. Curtains closed. Her show ended without nary a round of applause.

***

Naked as the day she was born, Angelique laid atop Poppa's rickety dining room table. Two pillows beneath her stomach provided a small degree of comfort.

Her arms were stretched behind her head. Nylon rope bound her hands to the refrigerator's door handle. Her bra combined with Poppa's wife beater to secure her ankles to the table's legs, spreading hers in the process.

"I'm really into kinky sex, but I don't think this table will support me," she stated drunkenly.

Mesmerized, Poppa stared into her pink void. Playing gynecologist, he used two fingers of his right hand to probe her wetness. His left hand freed his throbbing member from the confines of his boxer briefs. Angelique gasped at the sight.

He walked around the table, stopping directly in front of her. "That looks delicious," she giggled. "Let me taste it."

Poppa continued to stroke himself as if he were alone on the planet. "I know a few tricks you'd enjoy," she flicked her tongue seductively. "I'm horny. Put it in."

Tempting indeed, but Poppa knew he couldn't fulfill her wish. Watching her gyrate her hips, he felt his manhood stretch in his hands.

"In a minute," he managed to grunt.

Poppa reached around her left side to retrieve a black nylon bag, recently deemed to be his murder kit. Inside, he kept the nylon cord he'd used to strangle Gloria.

Angelique took it all in curiously. "What's that for? I'm already hogtied," she referenced the cord dangling from his right hand.

Poppa stood. His eyes glazed with a distant nobody's home stare.

"Poppa," worry dominated Angelique's tone. "Poppa," she attempted to get through.

"Poppa. You're scaring me," she began to struggle against her binds.

Entranced by visions of Gloria's body going limp, as he held her up with the cord looped around her neck, didn't allow a response from Poppa

"Poppa. Untie me. I'm not having fun."

Poppa walked into Angelique's blind spot. Her head swiveled. She strained to bring Poppa into view.

"What are you doing?" her worries turned to panic.

Slipping the cord around her neck, Poppa cooed in her left ear. "Shh!"

"Poppa, please. What are you doing?"

Poppa tightened his grip on the cord, cutting off Angelique's oxygen supply simultaneously.

"I wanna weave," she choked out.

"You'll never leave, my Angel. Tonight will bond our souls for eternity," he loosened his grip momentarily.

"Poppa, you're hurting me!" Angelique panted, sucking air into her lungs.

"No Mami. I'm killing you," Poppa jerked on the nylon cord.

Angelique's body thrashed, resembling a fish out of water. Poppa's forearms bulged. His muscles fought to contain her death throes. Her movements ebbed. In mere seconds, Angelique lay completely still. Her demise induced Poppa's climax.

Gratified, Poppa stared down. His ability to create life oozed from the tip of his swollen member, while his capacity to take life returned to its maker at his feet.

CHAPTER 12

"I called your house a hundred times, if I called once," Zy'kia blinked lime green L.E.D. lights into focus, 4:37 a.m. "Then I was like, dummy! Call his cell, duh!"

Happy? Zy'kia prayed he was in the midst of a bad dream.

"Our friend struck again last night," Happy's declaration confirmed his reality. "Beach patrol discovered the Vic twenty minutes ago. On Okaloosa Island. A quarter mile past Ramada Inn. Same side." The phone went dead in Zy'kia's ear.

Zy'kia glanced over at Leslie. *Still can sleep through a hurricane* he mused silently.

He kissed her forehead and left cheek, before slipping from the bed. Thoughts of the night they'd shared were quickly replaced by the killer's eerie whisper.

Have you noticed how terrified the good citizens of Okaloosa County are? They leave their homes and pray they make it back to them. Why? Because they don't have faith in your seventy-two percent either. They don't trust you.

Zy'kia gazed over at his gun and shield draped over a lawn chair's arm.

It's becoming obvious, that the oath you swore and the badge you wear are fraudulent.

Tugging on his shoes, Zy'kia's temperature began to rise as he thought.

People are burying their loved ones. And you call it a game? He eased his weight off the air mattress, doing his best not to disturb Leslie's sleep.

"This is exactly why I didn't give you any last night," Leslie's voice sounded in Zy'kia's left ear. "I knew you'd hit and run."

"You didn't give me any because I didn't try to get any. You know hit and run isn't my M.O. I'm more of the wham bam thank you ma'am type. But…" Zy'kia froze her response. "I'm leaving now because another body has been discovered," he draped his holster over his left shoulder, then slipped his badge over his head to dangle from a braided horsehair necklace.

"Do you think it's the same person that killed," Leslie exhaled audibly before saying, "Gloria?"

"I can't say as of now," Zy'kia turned to face her fully. "Gyps, I don't want to bring my job into this relationship, and right now I don't have time to discuss this any further. I have a murder scene to get to."

Leslie beamed inwardly. The knowledge of him considering them starting a relationship was reward enough. She'd see to capitalize on the opportunity to reclaim her lost love. "Will I see you later?" She gave in without a fight.

"Can't answer that either. I don't know how long I'll be dealing with this situation,' Zy'kia reached for the front doorknob.

"Let me get you a key."

Zy'kia rejected her offer by saying, "I'll call you."

Wordlessly, Leslie extended the thumb, index, and pinky fingers of her right hand. Swooping her hand forward she said, "It's a date."

Zy'kia allowed his attention to fall to an exposed thigh before copycatting her act. A giant smile was plastered to his face as he opened the front door, locked it, then closed it behind him.

***

Javid stood on the boardwalk next to the Gulfarium. He watched as several officers cordoned off the crime scene with yellow tape.

A crowd of onlookers loitered. He wanted to be closer but was fearful of being noticed, especially by Officer Curtis.

It'd been over an hour since the arrival of the first officer on the scene, and still, there wasn't any sign of Detective Blunt.

You don't have what it takes! He isn't thinking about you. He's probably following leads on the pretty Lil filly Poppa killed. You have a pack of mangy Labrador Retrievers out there chasing their tails. You ain't worthy to have a bloodhound sniffing behind you. The voices began to voice their opinions.

Some fox you are, Chip!

Slamming his fist down on the wooden railing, Javid hissed, "Leave me alone dammit!" Javid's eyes scanned his surroundings to see if anyone heard his outburst.

Do you need to look around to know you're alone? We're the only ones crazy enough to be near you. Anybody that's somebody, doesn't wanna be around a nobody!

"You'll see! Wait until the headlines," Javid attempted.

If she's so important, then where's Detective Blunt? The voices bottom-lined the topic.

***

Zy'kia steered his Ford Expedition behind the horde of official vehicles lining the side of Highway 98. Mel Stone, a reporter for The Playground Daily News, greeted him as he stepped down from the truck's cab.

"Morning detective," Mel fell in stride beside Zy'kia. "Think the murders are related?" Zy'kia activated the Expedition's alarm system. Its chirp served as his reply to Mel's question.

"Do you have any solid leads?" Mel continued his quest for information.

Zy'kia tried distinguishing the odd shapes of seashells he walked on as he progressed toward the beach.

"Detective, don't you think the public has the right to know?"

Cutting Mel off with a menacing glare, Zy'kia spoke through gritted teeth, "I don't think. I know. Someone's loved one is lying out there. When they shouldn't be. I don't know if it's a murder victim, or if their death was due to natural causes. But I do know there's a body over there." He pointed in the direction of the officers milling around.

"I remember sand skiing on these very dunes as a kid. Were you here when these suckers were a couple of stories high? Look at them now, barely six feet. Another eight to ten years, all of this will be flat as the seashore."

Catching Zy'kia's hint, Mel relinquished his questioning. "I remember them well. They were beautiful works of nature. And it's nature that's destroying them. Hurricanes and erosion." Mel's rebuttal signaled his willingness to play by Zy'kia's rules.

The hard gravelly mix of seashells and rocks soon gave way to sugar-white beach sand. Their feet sank deeply with every step.

Approaching the body, Zy'kia hit his brakes. "Mel, I've been reading your reporting since junior high. I feel you're good at what you do. That's why, if, and when, there's a statement to be made. I'll make it to you. Now if you'll excuse me. I have a job to do."

"Need I say more?" Happy used his right index finger to direct Zy'kia's eyes to a single Lays potato chip bag.

"So much for natural causes," Zy'kia mumbled under his breath before the killer's voice echoed in his head.

Do you know why I didn't stop after the first victim? Killing is like eating Lays potato chips. You can't stop with just one.

"Any I.D. on the body?"

"No. Curt did backtrack her route, and he believes the beige Mitsubishi Galant is hers. It's registered to a Kandra Harrison."

Settling on his haunches, Zy'kia lifted the white sheet covering the latest murder victim.

"There aren't any signs of struggle. No visible cause of death," Happy narrated as Zy'kia visually examined the body.

"I'm willing to bet a year's pay against a day's, that her system is flooded with insulin."

Rising, Zy'kia asked, "Any witnesses?"

"No one's come forward."

73

"Y'all may want to sit down for this," Officer Curtis swiftly strode in their direction. "Just got a call about another body. Apparent strangulation." Zy'kia and Happy exchanged bewildered looks.

"That ain't even the half of it," Curt continued as if that bombshell was a dud. "It's the sheriff's daughter, Angelique."

"Angelique. Angelique?" Happy asked.

"Angelique," Curt responded.

"You mean she's the one that discovered the body?"

Curt answered Happy's question by shaking his head. "How about, she is the body."

***

Javid stood on the boardwalk next to the Gulfarium. He watched as several officers cordoned off the crime scene with yellow tape. A crowd of onlookers loitered. He wanted to be closer but was fearful of being noticed, especially by Officer Curtis.

It'd been over an hour since the arrival of the first officer on the scene, and still, there wasn't any sign of Detective Blunt.

You don't have what it takes! He isn't thinking about you. He's probably following leads on the pretty Lil filly poppa killed. You have a pack of mangy Labrador Retrievers out there chasing their tails. You ain't worthy to have a bloodhound sniffing behind you. The voices began to voice their opinions.

Some fox you are, Chip!

Slamming his fist down on the wooden railing, Javid hissed, "Leave me alone dammit!" His eyes scanned his surroundings to see if anyone heard his outburst.

Do you need to look around to know you're alone? We're the only ones crazy enough to be near you. Anybody that's somebody, doesn't wanna be around a nobody!

"You'll see! Wait until the headlines," Javid attempted.

If she's so important, then where's Detective Blunt? The voices bottom-lined the topic.

***

Zy'kia steered his Ford Expedition behind the horde of official vehicles lining the side of Highway 98. Mel Stone, a reporter for The Playground Daily News, greeted him as he stepped down from the truck's cab.

"Morning detective," Mel fell in stride beside Zy'kia. "Think the murders are related?" Zy'kia activated the Expedition's alarm system. Its chirp served as his reply to Mel's question.

"Do you have any solid leads?" Mel continued his quest for information.

Zy'kia tried distinguishing the odd shapes of seashells he walked on as he progressed toward the beach.

"Detective, don't you think the public has the right to know?"

Cutting Mel off with a menacing glare, Zy'kia spoke through gritted teeth, "I don't think. I know. Someone's loved one is lying out there. When they shouldn't be. I don't know if it's a murder victim, or if their death was due to natural causes. But I do know there's a body over there." He pointed in the direction of the officers milling around.

"I remember sand skiing on these very dunes as a kid. Were you here when these suckers were a couple of stories high? Look at them now, barely six feet. Another eight to ten years, all of this will be flat as the seashore."

Catching Zy'kia's hint, Mel relinquished his questioning. "I remember them well. They were beautiful works of nature. And it's nature that's destroying them. Hurricanes and erosion." Mel's rebuttal signaled his willingness to play by Zy'kia's rules.

The hard gravelly mix of seashells and rocks soon gave way to sugar white beach sand. Their feet sank deep into the sand with every step. Approaching the body, Zy'kia hit his brakes.

"Mel, I've been reading your reporting since junior high. I feel you're good at what you do. That's why, if, and when, there's a statement to be made. I'll make it to you. Now if you'll excuse me. I have a job to do."

"Need I say more?" Happy used his right index finger to direct Zy'kia's eyes to a single Lays potato chip bag.

"So much for natural causes," Zy'kia mumbled under his breath before the killer's voice echoed in his head.

Do you know why I didn't stop after the first victim? Killing is like eating Lays potato chips. You can't stop with just one.

"Any I.D. on the body?"

"No. Curt did backtrack her route, and he believes the beige Mitsubishi Galant is hers. It's registered to a Kandra Harrison."

Settling on his haunches, Zy'kia lifted the white sheet covering the latest murder victim.

"There aren't any signs of struggle. No visible cause of death," Happy narrated as Zy'kia visually examined the body.

"I'm willing to bet a year's pay against a day's, that her system is flooded with insulin."

Rising, Zy'kia asked, "Any witnesses?"

"No one's come forward."

"Y'all may want to sit down for this," Officer Curtis swiftly strode in their direction. "Just got a call about another body. Apparent strangulation." Zy'kia and Happy exchanged bewildered looks.

"That ain't even the half of it," Curt continued as if that bombshell was a dud. "It's the sheriff's daughter, Angelique."

"You mean she's the one that discovered the body?"

Curt answered Happy's question by shaking his head.

"How about, she is the body."

***

Javid's demeanor swung one hundred eighty degrees as soon as he spotted Zy'kia trudging through the sand. He'd bask in his moment of glory and later enjoy his fifteen minutes of fame when the various media outlets broadcast his adventures.

The hound has arrived

Yeah, we're finally gonna be famous

Elation faded into confusion. Elated due to watching Zy'kia raise the white sheet to gaze down at his latest victim. One he knew had to be very important. Confused when seconds later Zy'kia and another detective began running away from his crime scene.

Perhaps they're going to inform the next of kin

Perhaps we're rollin' in the wrong head.

***

"Got damn it, Zy'kia!" Sheriff Norris unashamedly shed tears. "The sum bitch strangled her!" He banged his left fist onto the hood of his Dodge Intrepid. "My angel is gone back to heaven." Grief-stricken sobs overtook him.

Zy'kia felt the sheriff's pain. It intermingled with his own. Their pains were of different breeds. Yet, they were birthed from the same source.

The Fox.

Refusing to look himself, Sheriff Norris hooked a finger over his left shoulder. "Look at my baby," he croaked.

A solitary white sheet stretched out on the asphalt basketball courts of Edwins Elementary. "I want this asshole's head on my desk by breakfast! No courtroom. No judge. No jury. Straight execution! Don't give the prick a chance to get off on some B.S. technicality or get a rosy stay in a nuthouse. Shoot him on sight. And shoot to kill!"

Zy'kia's eyes rotated to engulf Happy's. Silently, they questioned whether they could grant the sheriff's desires. Were they able to murder on his behalf?

Zy'kia knew he wouldn't unless the situation demanded he do so. He'd trust the justice system. A deeper gaze into Happy's eyes left him uncertain of Happy feeling likewise.

***

Enjoying a bowl of his favorite Breyers Mint Chocolate Chip ice cream, Javid anxiously anticipated the start of the six o'clock news.

By the way, Zy'kia and the other detective rushed from the scene. He was certain his victim was special.

Impatiently, he waited through commercial after commercial. Finally, the promo for the six o'clock news.

"Good evening, ladies, and gentlemen. I'm Sue Vaughn, and this is the evening edition of W.E.A.R. Channel Three News.

Once again, tonight's top story takes us to Fort Walton Beach. The death toll in the recent string of murders has risen."

Scooping ice cream, Javid leaned forward in the rickety dining room chair he'd placed in front of the television.

"In what has left the entire county in shock and on edge. Today, shortly after 10 a.m. The remains of Angelique Norris. The daughter of Okaloosa's County Sheriff, Carlton Norris, was discovered by a group of.."

Unable to contain their excitement, the voices drowned out Sue's remarks.

I knew it! One screamed.

America's Most Wanted here we come

Javid helped himself to a celebratory scoop of ice cream. He smacked his lips, savoring the taste.

"Angelique's cause of death has officially been listed as strangulation," The reporter's announcement left Javid's right hand suspended in mid-air between mouth and bowl.

"Strangulation?" he questioned.

"Her remains were discovered on the basketball court of Edwins Elementary School."

"What? I didn't leave her on no damn ball court!" Javid screamed at the television. "I left her on the beach! Where I killed her!"

A picture of the victim filled his television screen. "That's not her!" Javid flung the remote controller across the room.

"Sheriff Norris was at the crime scene assisting investigators in the search for clues and gave our on-the-scene reporter the following statement." The view changed from Edwin's basketball court to Sheriff Norris standing in front of his Dodge Intrepid.

"My family and I are offering a hundred thousand dollars for information leading to the arrest of those responsible for the murder of our daughter, Angelique.

As a public servant, and a grieving father. I strongly encourage anyone with information to call the Okaloosa County tip line. I assure you that your identity will remain anonymous. Your call may save a life," Angelique's picture reclaimed the screen, causing Javid to become livid.

He slammed his bowl of ice cream down onto the ceramic tile flooring. Fuming, he stared at the TV.

"On Okaloosa Island," Sue Vaughn continued. "The body of Angela Bell was discovered by beach control early this morning. Investigators are attempting to determine whether the two murders are related. In other news,"

Javid leaped from his chair. He karate kicked the television off its stand.

"Do you think I'm going to let you steal my glory? **Poppa!**" Javid yelled.

The few remaining loose screws became unscrewed. He stomped the television unmercifully. "I'll kill you first. Swear to God!" he added drooling.

***

Poppa's swag levitated to higher levels. He felt on top of the world. The six o'clock news elevated his spirits. Indeed, he was the man. He'd beamed through the entire newscast.

This is cause for celebration. He turned his television off.

He hadn't felt any paranoia. No jitters. No fear of being caught. "I'm the boogeyman," Poppa pranced towards the front door.

"As a public servant and grieving father, I strongly urge anyone with information to call the police tip line," he mimicked Sheriff Norris. "Fuck chyou Mr. Sheriff, and chyou tip line."

***

Tired of watching Zy'kia pick over his shrimp-fried rice. Leslie asked, "Are you okay? In case you haven't noticed. I am here with you. You can talk to me."

Zy'kia sat his fork on the side of his plate. "I told you. I don't want to bring my job into this relationship." He pushed his plate aside and reached for his wine glass.

"Is that how you're gonna push me away also?" Zy'kia immediately recognized Leslie's pain by her tone.

"I understand you've had a rough day. Two murders, but what good can I be, if you don't allow me to be?"

Zy'kia emptied his glass in one fluid motion before speaking, "People are losing their lives because of me," he permitted his gaze to rest on hers.

"He called me. Yesterday, minutes before you called to invite me to dinner."

"Am I supposed to know who he is?"

"He, the killer." Zy'kia clarified. Leslie's hand flew upward to cover her mouth.

"I'm sure it was him. He made references that only the killer would know."

Leslie raised her glass. Zy'kia refilled his.

"This is a game to him," Zy'kia paused to wet his mouth. "A fox hunt. I'm the hound. He's the fox." Leslie drained her glass in three gulps.

"The rules of the game dictate people will continue to die until I catch him. The problem with that is I don't even know where to

80

begin. He's careful, Gyps. Very careful. He hasn't left a shred of worthwhile evidence at any of the crime scenes."

"He'll slip up sooner or later," Leslie attempted to stay positive.

"Yeah. But how many more will die before then? I don't have the luxury of waiting for him to slip up. Innocent people are losing their lives. Yet, my hands are pretty much tied until he does slip up."

Leslie stood, she walked behind Zy'kia and began to massage his shoulders. "I don't know what to say Zy'. I wish I could um…make it all go away somehow."

"You're doing a good job of it now." Zy'kia enjoyed her touch.

"I just want you to know that I am here for you. I love you, Zy'."

Zy'kia could sense the sincereness of her words. Feel it. Still, he knew words alone weren't enough. It'd require a miracle to cure his problems.

You aren't capable of protecting them. You aren't qualified. The killer's voice echoed inside his head.

CHAPTER 13

On Beal Parkway, Poppa crossed Gap Creek bridge. From a billboard, Angelique Norris smiled into every passing vehicle.

The word reward stood out in the background in bold letters, informing the public of the two hundred fifty-thousand-dollar reward being offered for information surrounding her death.

"Two hundred fifty thousand dollars? I may turn myself in for that amount of money," Poppa chuckled at his obvious joke.

Working alongside Javid, Poppa bragged on the billboard he'd seen on his way to the job site.

"Chyou need to see it, my friend. Can chyou believe it? The sheriff's daughter!"

The voices stirred. Javid seethed.

Yep. We're rollin' in the wrong head.

Poppa ran his trowel over the cement. He and Javid were finishing a driveway. On a roll, he continued.

"What a freak that one was amigo. She never knew I was death until it was too late." Into his craft, Poppa hadn't noticed Javid's angered expression.

"Please, Poppa. Untie me," Poppa imitated Angelique.

"Relax. I said to her. I'm not going to hurt you. I'm going to kill you," he narrated.

Javid had heard the recitation numerous times during the past week. He became more disgusted with each retelling. Nothing personal against Angelique. Poppa was his problem. For it was Poppa who'd stolen his glory.

At best, the death of Angela whatever her name was, could have received an honorable mention, in the wake of Angelique Norris'.

The sheriff's daughter? How do you top that? A voice pondered.

"The feeling of raw power was just…just…exhilarating." Poppa's voice invaded Javid's thoughts.

"To hear them beg and plead. It gives me an erection." Javid's eyes turned to slits as Poppa went on.

"Sex isn't the cure. Only death can satisfy my craving at this point."

He's stealing your joy and rubbing it in your face.

Cut his throat with your trowel, Chip.

Yeah. Let's see how exhilarating that is.

Gravel crunching under tires caused Javid to glance upward to see Zy'kia sitting in the driver's seat of his Expedition.

Oh shit, Chip! A voice exclaimed.

We're done Another one added.

That's one smart puppy, Chip!

Uh, guys. This is the scene where we run fox run.

"The way their bodies jerk as they fight for breath is like a skillful hand working to bring you to climax," Poppa admitted. "How 'bout you come the next time?" Poppa's back to Javid made him unaware of Zy'kia's presence.

Seconds passed without receiving an answer, Poppa spun. "Sweet Mary. Sweet mother of Jesus," Poppa whispered. For a fleeting moment, he locked eyes with Zy'kia.

He knows his job, Poppa. Javid's warning replayed. *Killing is the easy part, staying free is the task.*

Panic set in. Poppa's heart raced. His mind was a step behind. He'd seen Zy'kia's face on the news and in the papers. He knew whom he was gazing at. *I'm not going to jail.*

Poppa was pushing to his feet when the Expedition began slowly rolling backward.

That was a close one, Chip

***

Let's get outta here. He's calling for backup!

Poppa's eyes sought out Javid's, as he pretended to fuss over the concrete. Javid's attention focused on the Expedition backing into the driveway directly across from the one they were working on.

Yep Chip. He's setting up surveillance. We're dead! A voice noted.

Poppa repositioned himself to keep Zy'kia's Expedition in view. He resmoothed the concrete where the water bucket left indentions. His nerves were bad. His trowel and float trembled in his hands. Poppa forced himself to remain calm. He continued to work, listening for the sirens signaling the cavalry's rush.

Javid fought the voices for control. And won. He tried to work as if his greatest fear wasn't a stone's throw away. He glanced over at Poppa, noticing the sweat beads congregating on Poppa's forehead. Javid's nerves worsened.

Chip, if you know like we know. You'd run and take us with you.

***

Mentally weary, Zy'kia drove along Beal Parkway. Angelique's murder had taken a toll on the entire department.

The sheriff.

The mayor.

The City Council and every individual fancying themselves leaders were pressuring for the immediate apprehension of those responsible.

Unwilling to add stress, he'd chosen to isolate himself from Leslie. Yet, he longed for her comforting presence. Replaying their earlier phone conversation, he smiled.

"I don't care what time it is, Zy'," she'd said. "I want to see you tonight. The only choice you have in the matter is my place or yours?"

84

Realizing he wasn't holding a winning hand, Zy'kia folded by saying, "Yours."

The location was a no-brainer. With a deranged killer running around. He wouldn't dare allow her to venture out after dark.

Crossing Gap Creek Bridge, Zy'kia frowned as Angelique stared down from a billboard. The advertisement for a quarter of a million dollars was causing more harm than good.

The tip line phones were ringing non-stop, sending officers on an array of wild goose chases. A distress call for help had somehow become an attempt to win the lottery.

Zy'kia turned onto his street, Echo Circle. He fantasized aboout the temporary reprieve, a hot shower would render. It'd be a welcomed escape from the realm of stress he'd been circumferenced in since the murder spree began.

The two men working on the driveway of the house being built across the street didn't attract his attention. It was the Mazda pick-up that piqued his curiosity. He idled in the middle of the street trying to finger the importance of the Mazda.

Neither of the men's faces registered, but there was something about the truck. Giving up trying to piece the pieces of the truck's mystery together. Zy'kia shifted the Expedition into reverse and backed into his driveway.

***

Javid watched the Expedition as it backed away. *He's not a hound, Chip!*

Yep, he's a mutt!

Here's the fox! Fetch boy, fetch.

Their celebrating stopped abruptly. Zy'kia's truck didn't leave. It merely backed into a driveway across the street. Zy'kia exited his Expedition under Javid's watchful stare.

Now we know where the doghouse is, Chip!

Look at Poppa. He's scared.

Yeah, probably ready to tell.

Cut his throat Chip. Put the weakling out of his misery.

Javid found pleasure in Poppa's obvious fear. Thoughts of how Poppa was stealing his glory fluttered. He understood Poppa's emotional change. He fought his own minutes previously. Still, jealousy and envy prevented any feelings of sympathy.

"You still wanna go out killing?" Javid teased. "Looks like you're the one about to die."

"Fifteen minutes and this will be dry," Testing the concrete, Poppa changed the subject.

Javid gazed across the street. He studied the landscape surrounding Zy'kia's home, downloading every tree and shrub to memory.

***

Poppa sat alone, downing shots of Tequila, watching the six o'clock news. A week after Angelique's death, her murder was a still a hot topic. He was aware of there being another killer. Who also created his own brand of terror.

Oftentimes, he'd sit and try to analyze the other killer's thoughts. He used himself as a guideline.

"They'd have to bring in the National Guard if we were able to join forces," Poppa said aloud.

Mentally, he erased the visions of blood and gore he'd painted. Javid became his focus.

I wonder why he's acting so… Poppa paused to find a word to fill in the blank.

How do you say? He ended his struggle with a giant gulp of Jose Cuervo as if the answer could be found within the fiery liquid.

He's jealous. He doesn't have the heart of a killer. Not bothering to refill his glass, Poppa began drinking straight from the bottle.

Drunkenly, he pushed to his feet, swaying on unsteady legs. Still, he continued his tirade.

Forget Ted Bundy. Who is Jeffrey Dahmer? Son of Sam? They're nobodies compared to me! I, Poppa, will be the most feared killer in American history!

CHAPTER 14

Zy'kia studied Gloria's autopsy reports. It confirmed her cause of death as strangulation. Jumping from the paper was the fact of male semen being found on her lower back region.

How could I have missed that? He wondered silently.

An N.C.I.C. criminal database check failed to locate a match for the DNA sample, resulting in a missed opportunity to identify the killer. He allowed his eyes to scan the length of the paper, contemplating how to take advantage of the DNA discovery.

The phone rang.

Once.

Twice.

Zy'kia peered at the cracked receiver, making a mental note to put in a work order.

Three times the phone sang its melody. At the beginning of the fourth, Zy'kia removed it from the cradle. "Homicide. Detective Blunt."

A brief pause.

"You say that like there's something to be proud of. Homicide. Detective Blunt." The killer's voice parroted his.

"Tell me, detective. Did Sheriff Norris crying like a little wuss make you proud? Or does having to tell parents that their daughter ain't coming home because I am not qualified for the job you entrusted me with make you proud?" Disbelieving the killer's arrogance, Zy'kia fumed.

"Oh, you're too proud to speak. What's wrong? Fox got ya tongue?" The killer followed with an eerie laugh.

"I'll get the last laugh," Zy'kia responded.

The laughing ceased instantly. "You'll do what?" the killer hissed.

"Idle threats will only serve to provide a number of citizens the opportunity to make headlines. Apologize for your stupidity or visit another crime scene within the hour."

Silence.

"Are you saying, Your pride is worth someone's life?" the teasing, mocking tone, gone.

The killer spoke firm and decisive. "Have it your way, detective. Be sure to remind the family of why their loved one is dead. Goodbye detec..."

"Wait!" Zy'kia yelled. "I. I apologize." He forced the words from his mouth.

Who said, You can't teach an old dog new tricks? A voice voiced.

Again, the killer's eerie laugh filled the airwaves. Again, it vanished in a heartbeat.

"Apology not accepted! In fact, your behavior through all of this has been completely unacceptable!" The killer's venomous pitch stung Zy'kia's ears.

"I'm the band director, detective. You will dance to my music. Do I make myself clear?"

"Yes." Zy'kia didn't hesitate.

"Very good. Puppy."

"Anything. Just don't hurt anyone else."

"In order for me to do that detective. You'll have to catch me."

Zy'kia became enraged recognizing the unmistakable click and dial tone. He slammed the receiver against his right thigh repeatedly. When his fury passed, the earpiece dangled helplessly from one wire cord. He'd need the work order sooner than he thought.

***

What are you going to do about Poppa, Chip? His kills get the front page. Yours don't make the gossip column.

Javid stood in front of his bathroom's cracked mirror. Water ran into the sink. For thirty minutes the voices had been harassing him.

Agree to make a kill with him. Then cut his throat!

Play bitch and snitch Another voice echoed.

No, kill him! Let's see how powerful he is with a heart full of insulin.

He's a pain in the ol' kisser roo, Chip. You should stick him there.

Javid slapped his hands over his ears. The voices persisted.

Careful Chip. You're bound to knock the loose screws out. You know you're not wrapped too tight.

"Aaahh!" Javid screamed. "Stop! You're driving me crazy!"

Driving you? You came into this world riding the short bus!

We'll never make C.S.I. like this. We'll be forced to watch episodes about Poppa. Is that what you want?

Javid splashed water on his face. "Please. Just leave me alone. That's all I want. Just leave me alone."

Please. Just leave me alone. The voices echoed in a whiny tone.

He's a wuss. Let him be, guys. Before he breaks and we end up back in the crazy house.

Javid slumped to the floor and curled into a fetal position.

***

"You have to relax for this to help." Leslie paused massaging Zy'kia's shoulders.

"To be honest, Gyps. Catching this prick is the only thing that'll help," Zy'kia retorted.

"I thought we were making progress with the DNA sample found on Gloria's body. Then the killer calls to remind me that we're really stuck on first base unless he voluntarily provides a sample. No one believes in the likelihood of that happening.

Without him being arrested for another violent crime, his DNA won't ever be inputted into the criminal database, making the sample taken from Gloria's body about as helpful as…"

"You not relaxing while I'm trying to massage your shoulders," Leslie finished Zy'kia's statement.

"Wasn't what I was gonna say, but I guess it'll do." Zy'kia glanced over his shoulder, flashing her a smile. She replied with a slap to the back of his head.

"Relax Zy'. I'm not playing." Leslie warned. "Did you tell him about the DNA sample?" She resumed massaging.

"I didn't have the chance to say much of anything. I let my pride outweigh my better judgment," closing his eyes, Zy'kia enjoyed Leslie's therapeutic touch.

"Over to the left a little," He said then continued.

"He wounded my ego, Gyps."

"I received a call today myself." Zy'kia's eyes popped open.

"How did he get your phone number?" he asked seriously.

"How did he get my number? Well, I am the mother of his children. Technically, I'm still his wife."

"Huh?"

"Ron. Zy. Ron called."

"Oh," Zy'kia patted his right shoulder signaling Leslie to continue massaging.

"Another guy is trying to steal your girl and all you can say is oh?" Leslie's adding extra pressure caused Zy'kia to flinch.

"My girl. His wife. Who's the biggest winner? Do you want to tell me what he said or argue? I'm cool with one, but I don't have the time nor energy for the other," losing the vibe Zy'kia ended the massage session by standing up.

"He wants to reconcile for the children's sake."

"And?" Zy'kia ignored the crazy look Leslie forwarded in his direction.

"And what do you think, Zy'kia? I left because I was unhappy and tired of pretending. I left because I am still in love with you."

she peered over at Zy'kia. "I informed him divorce is the best for everyone including the children." Tears began to stream from her eyes. "He wants the children Zy. My babies."Leslie's obvious anguish broke Zy'kia's heart. It panged.

He knew no logical combination of words would make a difference. Therefore, he remained silent to ensure not to disrespect the severity of her dilemma. Zy'kia simply outstretched his arms, inviting her to take advantage of their comfort. No prodding required. She fell into them."What am I going to do Zy? They're my babies! I don't want to subject them to a messy divorce, and I darn sure ain't living without them." Leslie pounded a feeble fist into Zy'kia's chest. "Is wanting to be happy asking for too much?"*How did I get myself into this?* Zy'kia asked himself as Leslie's sobs became more intense. *First, a killing spree appears seemingly on a gust of wind. Now the love of my life seems to be forbidden.* Pulling her closer, he added. *"Lord, help us all."*

CHAPTER 15

"The city of Fort Walton Beach will hold an emergency city council meeting tomorrow night at six o'clock in the Fort Walton Beach High School's gym. The meeting will have its regular members along with Sheriff Norris and head detective, Zy'kia Blunt. They'll be on hand to field questions. The public is strongly encouraged to attend. According to Sheriff Norris, the meeting is to garner information as well as a solution to apprehend the person or persons responsible for the recent wave of murders." Javid relaxed on his couch eating a Washington red apple. *There's your chance for glory, Chip.* Javid watched the television as Sue Vaughn's face faded into a commercial. *You can see how they're planning to catch us. Yeah! Then we can stay a step ahead. The hound will be there.* Another voice added. *It'll be a thrill to be in their faces. Under their noses.*

***

Zy'kia studied the lab report detailing the specifics of Gloria's death "It's being replaced," he answered the question Happy's eyes asked. Happy gazed a minute longer at Zy'kia's destroyed phone without further inquiry. "Did you read this?" Zy'kia asked, sliding the toxicology report across his desk. "Not word for word," Happy reached for the papers. "I did glimpse it though." "Somehow we all missed a valuable find. Male semen was found on Gloria's lower back region." A smile began to form on Happy's features. "No match." Zy'kia erased it. "The ex-husband?" Happy wondered out loud.

"I'm going to ask him to provide a sample." "Does Sheriff Norris know about this?" "Yes," Zy'kia nodded his head to support his answer. "He had me in his office bright and early. Took more than a bite of my backside too." Happy laughed. "This is far from a laughing matter. People are losing their lives, including the sheriff's daughter. What it is- is a lack of competence on all our parts.," Zy'kia's forehead showcased angry wrinkle lines."Let's say, we could have found a match in the system. Our mistake would have cost two lives. Angelique's one of them.Overlooking the obvious is inexcusable, especially when at least fourteen eyes overlooked it." Making his point, Zy'kia had Happy resembling a school kid about to be sent to the principal's office."I don't know about you, but I don't find pleasure in failing the community. I didn't call you in here to give you a good reaming, nor are you here to pretend this issue is anything other than extremely serious." Zy'kia continued. "I'm to blame just as much as anyone else. I took full responsibility with Sheriff Norris. I also ensured him that something like this will never happen again," Zy'kia paused. He used his tongue to wet his lips. "Are you aware of the emergency city council meeting tonight?" Not trusting his voice, Happy nodded."It isn't mandatory that you attend," Zy'kia's tone softened. "But I, personally believe it'd be helpful if you did. Some valuable information may be unveiled. If nothing else, we can get a sense of where the public stands. The sheriff wants to reveal the discovery of the DNA. I strongly disagree. What's your take detective?"

***

"Perhaps another time, mi amigo. Tonight, I have a date with una bonita senorita," Poppa lied. "Have fun. Buenos noches," he pressed end to disconnect the call with Javid.*Why would I want to attend a city council meeting where the police are guests of honor?* Poppa peeped at the bottle of Jose Cuervo on the table next to his cellphone. Succumbing to cravings for the fiery alcohol, Poppa poured himself a drink.*Just a taste* Poppa reminded himself. He'd been drinking more than ever. It started as the alcohol providing courage. It progressed into him drinking because he lacked the willpower to say no to the cravings.Refilling his glass, Poppa spoke out loud. "Jose Cuervo is un malo hombre!"Javid chose a row of bleachers directly in front of the folding chairs housing Sheriff Norris, Detective Blunt, and the entire city council. Although the gym was nearly packed to capacity, people continued to file through the door.He took note of the W.E.A.R. Channel Three news contingent huddling around Sue Vaughn, the anchorwoman from the nightly news. "Excuse me," a middle-aged white woman said after stepping on his left foot. He smiled in acceptance of her apology.*Stupid Bi..Hey!Well, she should watch where she's going!*"Mind if I sit here?" Javid glanced up to see an overweight black lady standing in the aisle.*Where does she think, her big behind is going to sit?* A voice interjected."Not at all," Javid inched to his left. The gym filled to standing room only. Javid recognized officer Curtis leaning against a wall talking to a detective that appeared wildly familiar.*That's the mutt that's always with the hound at the crime scenes.* A voice informed."Honey, I will be glad when they catch the S.O.B. I haven't had a fresh-made donut since the beginning of the murders. Believe me, when I say, Mr. Donuts makes the best donuts in the south! Oh, baby! Theys brings a fresh batch out every day at eleven." She smacked her lips as if she could taste them. "If I had me a big, strong man such as yourself. I'd go get me some donuts anyways." She batted her eyes at Javid."You'd escort me to Mr. Donuts wouldn't you suga?"*I wouldn't take you to get donuts. But I would take your big ass to Jenny Craig.* The voices all supported that suggestion."If everyone will please come to order, we'll get started." Sheriff Norris' voice boomed through the gym's P.A. system. Javid focused his attention on the series of folding chairs, ignoring the woman's question."It's about time!" An angry male shouted.

"How many more must die?" another chimed.

"Fort Walton is just so big! Why hasn't the culprit been arrested?"

Sheriff Norris sat behind his microphone listening to the citizens vent their frustrations. "You and your entire police force are a waste of taxpayer's money."

"Especially Detective Blunt! All those decorations and he can't make me feel safe in my own home."

The latter statement manufactured a smile on Javid's face. The voices slapped hands and gave each other high fives. Javid peered at Zy'kia. The comment's sting registered on his face. *We may have to put the poor hound to sleep.* A voice noted.

"Ladies and gentlemen, this isn't a forum for you to ridicule our law enforcement. They're doing all in their power to apprehend the responsible party. The purpose of this meeting is to provide support and any information that may assist them in doing their jobs."

"Your attitude wouldn't be so nonchalant if you'd buried a loved one before their time," a woman's voice interrupted.

"Try burying your child. Then talk to me," another followed.

"Must I remind you of Sheriff Norris' daughter, Angelique, also being a victim?" Sylvia defended.

"Rightly so, seeing how the murders are a direct result of the job he's doing as sheriff. I find comfort in knowing I didn't waste my vote on him!"

Beat to silence. Councilwoman Sylvia Weatherspoon leaned back from the microphone in front of her as another woman stood to speak.

"My Angela's body was discovered the same day as his Angelique's," a sturdy index finger singled out Sheriff Norris. "My Angela was no less important. She had friends and family that loved and cared for her too. She was a good girl. My Angela. Straight A student. She was only home to protect me, but I couldn't protect her."

Javid turned to view the speaker. A petite black woman in her mid to late forties stood behind a microphone four rows above him and to his left. She clutched a framed picture to her bosom. "My

Angela's death," she continued. "It didn't receive attention. It was like she didn't matter. You," the accusing finger rotated towards Councilwoman Weatherspoon. "You would dare remind us of the sheriff losing a loved one? I am here to remind you that I lost my Angela. I can assure you that our grief is no less than his," once again Sheriff Norris became the main attraction. "But there are no billboards. No rewards for my Angela. Nor for any of the loved ones all these families have buried."

The gym had become church house quiet. The lady brushed away a tear while inhaling deeply. Exhaling, she went on. "I wonder if there'd even be a meeting tonight if his daughter hadn't been killed?" her eyes sought out the sheriff's eyes. He refused to meet her gaze by keeping his head lowered.

After realizing that Sheriff Norris wasn't going to acknowledge her presence with eye contact, she slumped down onto the bleachers. Angela's picture remained on her bosom.

We should kill her, *Chip. Put her out of her misery and let her be with her Angela.* The voices started.

We'd be doing her a favor.

This isn't even about you, Chip! They're honoring Poppa. And since we're here. We are too! You loser!

He stole your fame. Your glory. Insanity's right. You're such a loser!

Javid slapped his hands over his ears. He shook his head violently. The plus-size woman beside him glared in Javid's direction. "You okay sweetie?" she asked.

"Yeah," Javid grunted. "Sharp pain of an oncoming migraine."

"Lord, I tell you! Baby! I know bout those! Lucky you, I have the cure for it." She dug into her purse. Her search ended with her extending a bottle of Ibuprofen. "Two of those Lil darlings and you'll be feeling better directly."

Let's get some! We can get laid for a dozen donuts! Heck, I'll even spring for them!

I smell vagina. And it smells an awful lot like you Chip!

Happy to be away from the reporters and their cameras and microphones Zy'kia recalled the first interview he'd ever given. He was in the eighth grade, at Bruner Jr. High, and a reporter from the school's newspaper interviewed him after a basketball game.

"If everyone will please come to order, we'll get started." Sheriff Norris' voice boomed through the gym's P.A. system, ending his trip down memory lane.

"It's about time!" An angry male shouted.

"How many more must die?" another chimed.

"Fort Walton is just so big! Why hasn't the culprit been arrested?

He'd expected the citizens to state their concerns. Perhaps offer suggestions on catching the killer. The anger being displayed took him by surprise. He looked over at Sheriff Norris as someone new began speaking.

"You and your entire police force are a waste of taxpayer's money."

"Especially Detective Blunt! All those decorations and he can't make me feel safe in my own home."

Zy'kia uploaded memories of his playing high school basketball in this very gym. The cheers and applause he received yesterday replaced today's scorn and ridicule. *Many of these people probably used to cheer for me.* He thought.

"Ladies and gentlemen," Zy'kia scanned the crowd as Councilwoman Sylvia Weatherspoon began speaking. He recognized several faces from school. He spotted Carmen, sitting next to a face that seemed oddly familiar.

"The purpose of this meeting is to provide support and any information that may assist them in doing their jobs," Councilwoman Weatherspoon continued.

He's one of the guys that poured the driveway across the street! Zy'kia placed the face.

"Your attitude wouldn't be so nonchalant if you buried a loved one before their time," a woman interrupted.

"Try burying your child. Then talk to me," another followed.

"Must I remind you of Sheriff Norris' daughter, Angelique, also being a victim?" Sylvia defended.

"Rightly so, seeing how the murders are a direct result of the job he's doing as sheriff. I find comfort in knowing I didn't waste my vote on him!"

"My Angela's body was discovered the same day as his Angelique's," a sturdy index finger singled out Sheriff Norris. My Angela was no less important. She had friends and family that loved and cared for her too. She was a good girl. My Angela. Straight A student. She was only home to protect me, but I couldn't protect her." The gym fell silent. All eyes gathered on a woman clutching a framed picture to her chest. "My Angela's death," she continued. "It didn't receive attention. It was like she didn't matter. You," the accusing finger rotated towards Councilwoman Weatherspoon. "You would dare remind us of the sheriff losing a loved one? I am here to remind you that I lost my Angela. I can assure you that our grief is no less than his," once again Sheriff Norris became the main attraction. "But there are no billboards. No rewards for my Angela. Nor for any of the loved ones all these families have buried."

Zy'kia recognized her as the mother of the young lady found on the beach. The lady brushed away a tear while inhaling deeply. Exhaling, she went on. "I wonder if there'd even be a meeting tonight if his daughter hadn't been killed?"

Seeing her gaze pivot to Sheriff Norris, Zy'kia did the same. The sheriff diverted his eyes to the table, refusing to meet the woman's glare.

Zy'kia pondered over her statement. *Would there have been a meeting?* He questioned. Ashamed of the answer he'd concluded, he ventured on into deeper contemplation.

Where were the newspaper ads, billboards, and rewards for the other victims? They hadn't received any special media coverage. Regularly scheduled programs weren't interrupted to announce their passing. He sympathized with the sheriff's loss, but his loss wasn't more important than any other. Therefore, he wouldn't receive special treatment.

The woman's testimony invoked a somber mood. The taunts ended momentarily. Zy'kia considered the reprieve as an opportunity to make progress. He began speaking.

***

Javid swallowed the two Ibuprofen under the lady's watchful stare. "Give them a few minutes and you'll be feeling better than ever," she added a wink.

Who cares if she's plump? When's the last time we enjoyed our rib?
Let's get some, Chip.

Zy'kia's rich baritone filled the gym, chasing the voices to the back of Javid's head. "I'm here as a concerned citizen. That's first and foremost. As you all may know, I am the head detective of the Fort Walton Beach Police Department, and the lead detective on the recent string of murders," his words caused a few murmurs, but no one voiced an opinion.

"I personally guarantee each and everyone here that all is being done to bring the responsible parties to justice."

"If I catch 'em snoopin' round my family, I'm issuing the Cadenhead brand of justice. And I guarantee you we won't worry bout 'em beatin' the system on a legal technicality." A white guy wearing a National Rifle Association sweater promised.

"Sir that's exactly what we don't need. Citizens taking the law into their own hands." Zy'kia retorted.

"That's where you're wrong at. We're not safe with the law being in your hands!" the guy shot back. "Our streets are killing grounds. Everyone's looking over their shoulders. And you're standing here promising promises. We need more than empty guarantees. Me and some buddies are figurin' on startin' us a vigilante brigade. Our hands won't be tied by legal mumbo jumbo, and we feel we can get results that away."

"Sir, that's not the kind of assistance we're asking for," Zy'kia tried to reason.

"And this ain't the kinda life I want for my family but were living it." The guy was beyond reasoning.

"Carrying a concealed weapon without a permit is against the law," Zy'kia tried a different angle.

The man turned towards a group of men sitting slightly to his left. "Reckon that means we won't be concealin'" em fellas," he said earnestly. Redirecting his attention to Zy'kia, he added. "The constitution of the good ole U. S. of A. provides us the right to bear arms and by God, we're gonna bear em!" The gym erupted. A smattering of rebel yells wafted into the rafters. Riding the wave, he awarded Zy'kia his best 'so there' look.

"I am telling anyone that wishes to openly break the law. You will be arrested on sight." Zy'kia countered with a how do you like them apples gaze.

"I think it's absolutely the brightest of dumb ideals!" the guy wasn't quite done. "He's willing to lock us up for protecting our family and property. While they allow a killer to prey on the community. Do y'all hear this?" he pivoted sixty degrees left. Then forty-five right. "Guess you ought to keep a light on for me. If I can go cross seas to other countries to fight for freedom, I damn sure can fight to keep my backyard safe." A solid round of applause reverberated. "Detective," the man paused for the applause to end.

"Detective, I'm bout as ornery as a fresh woke grizzly in the middle of hibernation. And that, sir. Doesn't make me the friendliest person on God's earth. I hear, don't engage. Blah. Blah. Blah. The suspect is armed and dangerous. Yadda. Yadda. Dee. Well by golly I am armed and dangerous too!" The ensuing roar held the assembly hostage for ninety seconds.

Sheriff Norris paid the ransom. "Ladies and gentlemen, I'll be the first to admit. I totally understand your feelings and concerns." "Well put the donut down and get off youse arses and make us safe again," an elderly snowbird yelled. Sheriff Norris cleared his throat.

Continuing, he said. "The perp or perps hasn't given us anything to help our cause. He's careful. Very careful. History says crime scenes that are squeaky clean equal the crime was committed elsewhere. My daughter's murder is an example," murmurs of displeasure riffled.Undeterred Sheriff Norris proceeded without caution. "We were able to obtain a DNA profile from one of the victims. We're awaiting a match in the N.C.I.C. database. Thus far we haven't been successful in obtaining a match, but we will. And when we do.."

"Don't start making promises! You haven't delivered any of the ones you made during your campaign." An angry voice shut the sheriff down.

Javid sat up straighter so as to not miss a word coming out of Sheriff Norris' mouth. His eyes swiveled to include Zy'kia in his visual picture. He was happy to see a painful expression dominating Zy'kia's features. It was evident. The hound didn't agree with the sheriff spilling the department's secrets.

Javid concentrated. Mentally, he uploaded every murder he'd committed. After several seconds spent contemplating, he was satisfied that he hadn't left such incriminating evidence.

Did you hear that, Chip? Poppa and his pea brain have given us a get-out jail-free card. The voices drowned Sheriff Norris out.

If the DNA doesn't match, you must unlock the hatch! Several voices chanted.

"We're investigating every lead that comes into the tip line. Due to the lack of time and manpower. We're not able to get to them all as quickly as we'd like, but we're going to get to them. The public's cooperation is greatly needed, welcomed, and appreciated," Sheriff Norris concluded.

Look at the hound, Chip. He reminds me of a sick puppy.

I told yall he was a cur. Did the sheriff ruin your investigation, puppy?

Let's give him something to do Chip. I say we kill the city councilwoman. That'll get us the headlines we deserve!

Yeah! Do y'all see her sitting there like she's all high and mighty? Like she ain't got a single care in the world.

I'm with BG. Let's bring her down off her high horse!

They're here figuring out how to catch a killer. No one has said a word about how not to let a killer catch them. You are a killer, aren't you?

Javid focused his attention on councilwoman Sylvia Weatherspoon. She sat straight-backed, with her head high, resembling royalty forced to rub shoulders with peasants.

Bring her down a notch, Chip! That'll be the only language she can relate to."

"Tonight, in Fort Walton Beach's High School gymnasium, concerned citizens gathered to express their desires and concerns to Sheriff Norris and other city leaders,"

Poppa sat sipping the one small drink that had miraculously manifested a variety of small others.

Alcohol made it difficult for Poppa to keep up with the news anchor. "The meeting," she went on. "Was interrupted throughout the night by angry outbursts by those in attendance," the view changed from the anchorwoman to a scene taking place inside the gym.

"Your attitude wouldn't be so nonchalant if you buried a loved one before their time!" a woman blurted through the television's speaker.

Poppa allowed his eyes to scan the crowd in search of Javid. "The purpose of this meeting is to provide support and any information that may assist them in doing their jobs," Councilwoman Weatherspoon declared.

I'll have to get Javid to fill the details in tomorrow at work. Poppa thought silently.

The news reporter continued with her report. "Things got heated when a citizen informed Detective Blunt of his intentions to create a vigilante brigade with several of his friends."

"Vigilante?" The reporter succeeded in capturing Poppa's undivided attention. He leaned forward not wanting to miss a word. The camera panned outward, filling the television screen with a redneck wearing a National Rifle Association tee shirt.

"If I catch 'em snoopin' round my family, I'm issuing the Cadenhead brand of justice." The man said boldly. "If I can go cross seas and countries to fight for freedom, I damn sure can fight to keep my backyard safe!"

Poppa downed the last of his Tequila as the man ended his statement. The anchorwoman's narration surrendered to the redneck's monotone, as the camera showcased his features in a widescreen view. He was the main attraction for a quarter minute, then the camera began to fade away from the would-be vigilante and returned to the anchorwoman sitting behind a desk in the newsroom.

"In a startling turn of events," she transitioned smoothly into her next topic. "Sheriff Norris dropped a bombshell on the standing-room-only audience.

The screen switched. Sheriff Norris became the star.

"The perp or perps hasn't given us anything to help our cause. He's careful. Very careful," Hearing the good news, Poppa reached for the bottle to pour himself a celebratory drink.

"We were able to obtain a DNA profile," Poppa's celebration was short-lived.

Poppa jerked his head up to stare at the television. The action caused him to miss his glass. He poured alcohol onto his coffee table.

"We're awaiting a match in the N.C.I.C. database."

Poppa hardly heard the remainder of the sheriff's statement. His heart raced and his hands trembled. "Stay tuned for more W.E.A.R. Channel Three news at ten."

Oh, snap! I hope the DNA came from a body the other killer killed. Poppa became frantic.

"Having legal problems? Let us provide a solution. The law firm of Sowell, Sowell, and Sowell specializes in all of your legal needs. For a free consultation, give us a call at 850-682-LGAL. That's 850-682-5425."

Poppa inserted the mouth of his Tequila bottle into his. *What the hell have I gotten myself into?* He mused as the fiery liquid burned its way to the pit of his stomach.

CHAPTER 16

Javid waited inside his 1994 Nissan Sentra. The car's heater died two winters back. White puffs of breath escaped through his nostrils. Councilwoman Sylvia Weatherspoon idled three cars ahead of him unaware of the clear and present presence of danger. Javid systematically patted the Sentra's gas pedal to keep it from stalling. The voices had him convinced that councilwoman Weatherspoon becoming a victim would catapult him into the limelight. Visions of headlines danced in front of his eyes as he waited for the light to change.

If the city leaders aren't safe, no one will be. The voices offered verbal encouragement.

We're going big time, Chip!

The light changed. Red became green. Javid's patting evolved into a downward press, sending the Sentra in pursuit of his prey.

She wanted to catch a killer. Let's see how she acts now that she's caught one, Chip.

Javid didn't attempt to shake the voices. Instead, he fed off their bravado, extracting encouragement and strength to complete his mission.

He agreed with the voices. Sylvia's status in the community guaranteed her death would send shock waves rippling from one end of the county to the other. Seeing Sylvia's Chrysler make a left off of Wright Parkway onto Deal Avenue, Javid turned on the Sentra's left turn signal and copycatted the act.

You'll have the hound howling at the moon after this one, Chip.

Javid spotted the Chrysler's right turn signal flashing Sylvia's intentions in the darkness. He completed his turn and then sped up, to make a right onto East Audrey Circle in time to see Sylvia pulling into the fourth house on the left's driveway.

He switched off the Sentra's headlights. The vehicle slowly rolled to a stop at the foot of Sylvia's driveway. *Da-da...Da-da..* The voices hummed the attack music to Jaws

Someone's in trouble!

Javid exited stealthily. He carried a bag of Lays in his gloved right hand. Councilwoman Weatherspoon's leaning into her backseat permitted Javid to continue his approach unnoticed.

We're gonna be the talk of the town come morning! The voices clamored.

Councilwoman Weatherspoon straightened herself up. Startled by Javid's presence, she dropped a briefcase from her right hand.

"Excuse me, Ms. Weatherspoon. Forgive me. I didn't mean to frighten you," Sylvia's eyes darted in their sockets.

They raced across the street before scurrying towards her front door. Realizing she was alone with a stranger, Sylvia determined to toughen up.

"How may I help you?" she asked minus the smug attitude displayed at the meeting.

"I want to do my part in helping bring the killer to justice. I wish to remain anonymous. For fear of retribution. I'm sure you understand." Thinking Javid to be a concerned citizen, her demeanor changed.

"I have information about the murders," by moonlight Javid saw her features brighten.

"Sir, I recommend you inform the police, or simply contact the tip line," Javid's head shook in disagreement.

"I want you to be my messenger."

Confused, Sylvia questioned, "Your messenger? A message for whom?"

Javid shuffled forward. "A message for those wishing to catch a killer. Nobody's safe. Tell the hound he can't protect them."

"Excuse me?" Sylvia stepped backward, hoping to provide distance between her and Javid. The body of her Chrysler limited her flight.

"You wanted to catch a killer, didn't you?" Javid closed in. "Did you ever consider the consequences of catching me?"

The usage of the pronoun me slapped reality into Sylvia's mind. Her eyes stretched.

"Please. I'll do whatever. I'll deliver your message to the mayor himself. Anything. Just please, don't hurt me."

"Hurt you? Why would I hurt you?"

"Aren't you the." Sylvia's inquiry ended on the tip of her tongue. Her eye was transfixed on the syringe dangling from Javid's left hand.

"Don't kill me," she whimpered. "I have money. I'll do anything. Just don't." Sylvia melted to the ground sobbing uncontrollably.

Now she wants to play 'Let's make a deal.' Well, what do we have behind door number one?

An overdose of insulin!

Yay. Yay!

And behind door number two, we have a beautiful brand-new casket!

Yay! Yay!

Javid towered over Sylvia as the voices continued their charade.

And finally, behind door number three we have just for you Sylvia. A customized billboard complete with reward and tip line information.

Javid allowed the bag of Lays to slip through his fingers. They landed on the ground beside Sylvia. *Give the old hag her prizes, Chip. And let's bounce!*

"Please! I'll," Sylvia desperately searched the darkness for help. None would be forthcoming. "Don't kill me." Her words came out in a harsh whisper.

Ramming the syringe deep into Sylvia's neck, Javid replied. "It's the only way for you to deliver my message."

Councilwoman Weatherspoon's left hand rested on Javid's right forearm. He extracted the syringe from her neck as she toppled over onto her left side. Her eyes were wide, staring into eternal darkness. Her soul raced to the pearly gates only to find out she was short several good deeds in the price of admission.

CHAPTER 17

"No need for me to ask why you didn't call me yesterday," Javid tossed the day's edition of The Playground Daily News newspaper at Poppa's feet. "I see you've been busy."

"I don't come to work yesterday because I have a giant headache. Much too much partying with la Senoritas," Poppa's curiosity induced him to reach for the newspaper.

The paper's headlines leaped from the front page. 'City councilwoman Sylvia Weatherspoon found slain in her driveway."

"I pray you were careful enough not to leave your DNA this time," Javid said sarcastically.

"But I didn't,"

"You're really rollin' now," Javid interrupted. "Tell me the details amigo. Did she beg for her life like the others?"

"I didn't take her life," Poppa spat.

"Come on, buddy. You can tell me. I'm your friend till the end."

"I'm serious amigo. I have never seen this puta," Poppa shook the newspaper as extra emphasis.

"Okay, whatever you say." Javid snatched the newspaper from Poppa's grasp. "But you should know. This article says the body is being swabbed for DNA evidence to compare to the sample they already have. I do pray you were careful," Javid sought out Poppa's eyes. Holding them with his, he included. "For your sake!"

"We know someone was committing the murders before me," Poppa squatted on his haunches. "It's his DNA that they have on file. Not mine." A key ingredient was absent from the statement.

Confidence.

Poppa understood that there was a great chance that his DNA was the one being discussed. He'd made the weak defense proclamation more so for self-consolation. Still, he didn't feel any better.

When he'd started killing, the thought of going to prison never entered Poppa's mind. Now the possibility of receiving life or the death penalty haunted him. In a matter of days, he went from feeling indestructible to becoming a nervous wreck.

"We're waiting for the lab results, but the M.O. fits the other victims. After Sheriff Norris' bright idea of revealing the DNA evidence. I'm sure the killer or killers will be taking extra precautionary measures. He made our job harder than it has to be." Maneuvering the Expedition through slower-moving traffic, Zykia glanced over at Leslie.

"Everyone's on edge. That's for sure. Watch that car!" Leslie warned watching an elderly gentleman change lanes unexpectedly.

"Do you think we'll see groups of vigilantes starting to roam the streets?" she asked once Zy'kia countered the old man's misstep.

"I wouldn't doubt it. But it is the last thing we need. A bunch of gun carriers with itchy fingers."

"It may be what's needed." Zy'kia looked at Leslie like she'd lost her mind. "I mean, no one is safe, Zy. First the sheriff's daughter. Now a city councilwoman? I don't want to imagine what he's planning as an encore," Leslie gazed out of the passenger's window into the face of Angelique Norris plastered to a billboard.

"Any useful information deriving from the tip line?" She inquired as they traveled across Gap Creek bridge.

"Naah Gyps. The information usually ends up being a wild goose chase," Zy'kia didn't bother masking his dejection.

"Keep at it, Zy. You'll get the break you need."

"Yeah, I'm sure. But how much bloodier will my hands be? That's the question." Unsure of how to respond, Leslie exercised her right to remain silent for the duration of their ride to Publix.

111

***

"Cheer up bro. I have a taste for Publix chicken. Come on. My treat." Poppa's eyes swept the drying cement.

"It's going to dry whether we're here or getting something to eat. To make you feel better. We'll put up boards to keep anyone from driving on it."

Javid and Poppa circled Publix's parking lot for the third time. "I swear I didn't kill that congress lady," Poppa declared.

"Councilwoman, amigo," Javid corrected. "You're still thinking about her?"

"No. No. I am thinking of you and how you don't believe my words," Publix's sliding doors slid open.

"I don't have to believe you. If the DNA is yours, he's the one you'll need to convince." Poppa's gaze drifted in the direction of Javid's head nod.

He nearly froze. Seeing Detective Blunt wasn't the cause for his initial reaction. It was the female standing next to him that had him mesmerized. She had to be without a doubt the most beautiful woman he'd ever seen.

Javid recognized the woman also. Her beauty stirred the voices.

Look at what the hound is keeping in his doghouse, Chip. They began.

No wonder he isn't sniffing behind you. He's busy trying to put pups in his bitch. The thought of Zy'kia thinking anyone more important than him created a jealous rage. On the way to the deli, Poppa asked. "Did you see the senorita, amigo? She looks like a movie star. A model at least. Wonder what she's doing with him?"

You have to kill her, Chip! Think about the headlines that'll bring. Detective Blunt's eye candy found sour. The voices found that hilarious.

I bet Poppa is already plotting to steal your joy.

Yeah! Poppa is a snake and can no longer be trusted!

We should kill him, too. My great grandmother always did say, 'onliest thing a snake's good fer is killin'

112

Javid turned to peer at Poppa. Noticing Poppa's attention elsewhere, he gazed in the direction to find Detective Blunt's lady friend rounding the corner of aisle seven. She held a box of Cinnamon Toast Crunch in her right hand. Fruity Pebbles filled her left.

See Chip! Told you. The voices screamed. *He's gonna screw everything up.*

"Planning on doing her, too?" Javid whispered his question.

"I was doing her, amigo! I was just about to fill her up with this. Until you ruined it for me!" Poppa tugged at his crouch.

Poppa smiled, but his intended humor sailed past Javid. Convinced Poppa wanted to steal his glory pushed him past laughing and joking.

At that moment, Javid's mind concluded. *Poppa must be dealt with. All those in favor say aye.*

Aye. Aye.

Hear ye. Aye. Continued to ring out until every voice in his head seconded his decision.

CHAPTER 18

"What you're saying is, I've become a suspect? Do you think I killed Gloria? While you're in here wasting both of our time and taxpayer's dollars, you should be in the streets, exploring tips, anything other than what you are doing!"

"No sir, Mr. Pride. I am not accusing you of murdering Gloria. This is standard procedure. The DNA sample will exclude you from the suspect pool." Zy'kia sat on a corner of his desk. Having rejected his offer of a seat, Mr. Pride stood.

"We're wasting time, detective. We're in here lollygagging and the killer is out there roaming free. Perhaps even stalking his next victim," wrinkles zigzagged across Mr. Pride's forehead, indicating his displeasure in being asked to provide a DNA sample.

"I apologize for any inconvenience, but this is necessary in order to allow us to focus our attention on finding the ones responsible. A simple swab of your mouth is all I need. Three minutes tops then you'll be free to leave."

Four minutes later, Mr. Pride extended a cotton swab toward Zy'kia saying, "Am I the only suspect? Nearly a month and.."

"As I've said earlier, you're not a suspect. And this," Zy'kia wiggled the swab. "Will keep you from becoming one." He failed to exclude his growing irritation from infiltrating his tone.

Picking up on Zy'kia's annoyance, Mr. Pride detoured. "You'll have to forgive me, detective. I understand you're doing your job. It's losing Gloria so suddenly and not having closure or answers to the million questions clouding my brain. It's all taking a toll on me. If there's anything else.." Zy'kia's desk phone began ringing interrupting Mr. Pride.

"Excuse me for one minute," Zy'kia said as he reached for the receiver. "Homicide. Detective Blunt speaking."

"Help me, detective! There's a fox in my henhouse and he's killing all my chickens," a desperate voice rushed into Zy'kia's ears seconds before the killer's sinister laugh.

"Hurry! Send the hounds!"

More laughter.

"At times I tickle myself, but not to death." Zy'kia glanced up to find Mr. Pride staring at him strangely.

"Is it a habit of yours to treat callers so rudely?"

Silence.

"Guess a few more bodies will loosen your tongue."

Zy'kia felt the heat of Mr. Pride's glare. Oddly, he tried imagining what he must be thinking. "I'll call you back in thirty minutes with information on where to send the meat wagon," the killer announced gaining Zy'kia's undivided attention.

"No! Wait!" Zy'kia blurted. "I mean, that won't be necessary. How can I help you?"

"That's more like it."

"I'm not alone. Is there a way we can continue.."

"Bodies are filling the morgue, and you're concerned with not being alone?" The killer laughed. "My don't we have our priorities in order, detective?"

Waving his hand, Mr. Pride mouthed the words, "Call me." Zy'kia responded with a thumbs-up.

Delaying until his office door closed behind Mr. Pride, Zy'kia asked, "Isn't there an alternative to spare the lives of the innocent civilians being harmed? Surely," the killer's laughter drowned out Zy'kia.

"You could simply stop today, and never be caught." Zy'kia finished.

"And what satisfaction would that bring you, detective? You'd have to live the rest of your life knowing that you failed.

Right now, you remind me of an incompetent prosecutor attempting to plea bargain with a killer. Disgusting to say the least.

At the city council meeting, everyone was so hellbent on catching a killer. Sylvia Weatherspoon was the unlucky one to catch me, and it literally thrilled her to death!" Zy'kia held the phone's receiver away from his ear to escape the killer's eerie laugh.

"No deal!" Anger battered Zy'kia's eardrums.

"Ordinary people will no longer suffer for the city leader's irresponsibility. From here on, the city leaders will be held accountable. You should know that. Didn't Sylvia deliver my message?" Silence filled the line as Zy'kia tried to decipher the killer's meaning.

"Message?" Zy'kia mumbled.

"Yes. Message. It was short and to the point, which is. You aren't qualified to protect them!" The line went dead in Zy'kia's ear.

***

Poppa couldn't shake the images from his head. For the past two days, he visualized her face. Her body. Her eyes. The elegance of her walk. It all combined to create an intoxicating nightmare. The woman from Publix dominated his thought process.

Poppa endeavored to wash away the visions with the potent fire water, Jose Cuervo. The more he drank. The more vivid his fantasies became. His loins ached with desire, due to his imagining her body convulsing in death throes. Then the headlines and terror that were sure to follow. The pressure grew in intensity. Searching for relief, Poppa unzipped his Wrangler jeans and began jerking the stress from his aching member.

***

"Clean." Zy'kia slid Gloria's autopsy report across his desk.

"Cause of death is strangulation. That gives us two methods; does that equal two killers or one with no particular method?"

116

Fearful of the consequences of missing details, Happy read the report in its entirety. "The ex-husband's DNA doesn't match the profile either." He added to Zy'kia's list of questions that needed answering. "And that leaves us exactly where we started. Nowhere."

Zy'kia studied Happy wondering if he should confide in him about the fact of the killer contacting him. Deciding against it, he inquired about the tipline. "Anything promising coming from the tipline?"

"Nothing worth talking about," Happy answered.

"There's been reports of vigilante groups patrolling neighborhoods after dark. Sylvia's murder has the city on edge. To the average citizen, everyone is a suspect." Happy reached for his pack of Marlboro Reds, remembering he was supposedly cutting back. He retracted his right arm.

"Soon there'll be an innocent person laid up in Fort Walton Beach Medical Center fighting for their life. The people want a tangible object, Zy'kia. Right or wrong. Guilty or innocent. They want someone to be held accountable."

Zy'kia agreed with Happy. He'd spent time before getting dressed thinking along the same lines. A slight head nod provided confirmation. "And what do you suggest?"

Happy paused to put his thoughts in order. "Suggesting is the easy part. The problems come in manifesting suggestions into reality,"

Another pause.

"Only one suggestion though and that's catch him."

Javid peered through high-powered Daily Summit Infrared Night Vision Binoculars that he'd purchased from the Army-Navy store on Beal Parkway. One hundred fifty yards and Zy'kia's front door seemed touchable.

For the past hour, he'd been waiting patiently, watching. Tonight, made the third this week without favorable results. Zy'kia wasn't his concern. His lady friend was. She'd made an impression.

A lasting one. He knew Poppa would definitely be on the hunt for such a trophy.

Kill him and be rid of the problem. The voices warmed up.

Javid resisted the voices' desires. To merely kill Poppa would be too easy. He had other plans for his dear friend. Not having the details worked out, Javid issued Poppa a stay of execution.

Headlights captured Javid's attention. His eyes followed a slow-moving car past Zy'kia's driveway into the one next door. "Where the hell is this dude?"

Javid briefly considered breaking into the house, but the risk simply for the thrill was far too great. He slipped out of the bushes he'd been nestled in. Making his way back to his Nissan Sentra, the voices offered consolation.

Tomorrow, Chip. There's always tomorrow.

Drunk. Intoxicated by bloodlust, Poppa cruised Miracle Strip Parkway, thirsty for the kill. Detective Blunt's mystery lady ignited a fire that required dousing.

He knew the chosen victim would be an unworthy substitute. Yet, she'd be good enough to be considered a fix. His hands longed to feel the struggle. The fear in their eyes. The desperate attempt to cling to life. The whoosh of their last breath.

There wouldn't be a method tonight. Color nor age mattered. Availability would be the determining factor in selecting his prey.

There she stood. Twenty yards away.

Tonya, the night shift duty officer stood in Zy'kia's office's doorway. "Hey," Zy'kia said glancing up. "You're here early."

"Beats being home alone. Plus pay. Sheriff Norris wants to see you in his office. Says it's urgent." Tonya lingered for another exhale as if she were battling within. Smiled, then did a textbook about-face.

"What now?" Zy'kia thought out loud.

His salty attitude derived from having his sleep disturbed at five o'clock this morning. Another body had been found.

The victim was a Mexican female in her mid to late twenties. She'd been strangled. Her remains were discarded inside an Environmental Waste dumpster behind Cash's Liquor Store on Okaloosa Island.

Zy'kia stifled a yawn. The murders were beginning to weigh on him. He felt guilty for being unable to prevent them.

Ashamed from knowing the innocent were being slaughtered because of a game. "Fox Hunt." The words left a disgusting taste.

Zy'kia shut off thoughts of the killer, and the murders in general. Wondering why Sheriff Norris wanted to see him took center stage.

Whatever it is, it can't be good. And by it being urgent, it means one thing. Disastrous.

Off to see the wizard, Zy'kia opened his office door.

The phone began ringing with his right hand still holding the doorknob. For a split second, he contemplated answering it but ditch the idea saying, "There's only so much bad news a guy can handle before noon.

You have to kill him, Chip.

Yeah! Before he messes everything up!

The voices were furious. *We can't let him beat us to the hound's flea catcher.*

I wish I was a flea!

Me too!

And me!

Really? As I was saying, Detective Blunt's lady friend is the biggest prize to be had.

We can't afford to let Poppa interfere with our destiny.

Javid couldn't resist further. He leaned on the bathroom sink, exhausted. Cold water dripped from his head. Denying the obvious wouldn't benefit anyone. Poppa was officially a hindrance. One that could no longer be tolerated.

He reflected on Poppa's call over an hour ago. His bragging about his latest victim. He'd explained in graphic detail until Javid pictured the victim and her struggles. As soon as they disconnected the call is when the voices started.

At first, Javid sympathized and made excuses for Poppa. Poppa was the only friend he'd ever had. Other than good ole Grams. Yet, the truth prevailed. Poppa had become a madman. Rabid from his initial taste of blood.

The time of Javid using Poppa's killings as motivation for him to choose better victims for himself had passed. Poppa's newfound obsession to kill Zy'kia's lady friend transformed Javid's self-proclaimed competition into an all-out race for glory. A race the voices had Javid determined to win by any means necessary.

Exiting the bathroom, Javid checked the hallway wall clock, 11:10 am.

Call the hound, Chip. Tell him you're tired of killing and you want to own up for your wrongdoings and want forgiveness.

Encouragement from the voices made Javid feel worse about betraying Poppa. As the age-old saying goes, everything has a price. Poppa was expendable.

The price for glory.

Javid removed his cell phone from his left front pocket. He pressed star six seven, to block his number, then proceeded to dial Zy'kia's office number. Listening to the phone ringing, Javid reflected on the good times he'd shared with Poppa.

"You've reached the office of Detective Zy'kia Blunt. I'm not available to take your call at this time. Please leave a detailed message along with your name, and phone number, and I'll return the call at my earliest convenience."

Beep!

Javid hung up without a word. Unbeknownst to Poppa, he'd received another stay of execution.

"Have a seat Detective," Sheriff Norris motioned toward the only empty chair in the room.

Zy'kia paused in the doorway. Two unfamiliar faces warranted his caution. He made his way to the offered seat, as Sheriff Norris introduced the visitors.

"Detective Blunt. Captain Winningham. I understand you two have spoken over the phone. And this is his superior, Major Madison." The trio exchanged head nods. Sheriff Norris went on, "The young woman who was murdered last night was one of theirs. Senior Airman Felicia Mendez." Zy'kia's mind fast-forwarded, attempting to predict where the conversation was heading.

"It took the killer to tamper with government property for Uncle Sam to take an interest." Sarcasm tainted the sheriff's words.

"We've been interested the entire time, Sheriff." Major Madison spoke. "We offered help at the start. But yes, Airman Mendez's death is the reason for us sitting here today. We protect our own."

Angered by the insinuation that he wasn't protecting the civilian population, Sheriff Norris mumbled, "Try telling Ms. Mendez's family that."

The two men spent the next quarter minute engaged in eye dagger warfare.

"The mayor is being squeezed by,"

Pause.

"Sam's boys. To find the killer or relinquish jurisdiction."

Zy'kia digested the information emotionless. Mentally he sized up the two servicemen, while Sheriff Norris continued to air his displeasure to his three-man audience.

"They lose one that would have been sacrificed on foreign soil for something that has absolutely jack to do with us, by the same Uncle, that is now acting like he gives a damn about her death. Bunch of hypocritical sons of bitches. That's what they are!" No one dared to speak. For fear of pouring gas on a raging inferno. "Two weeks, Zy'kia. That's the deadline. Trust me. I don't like it one bit, but my hands are tied."

Zy'kia hadn't ever been removed from a case. In a strange way, he relished the idea of passing on the stressful headaches to the government.

It's becoming obvious. The oath you swore and the shield you wear are fraudulent. You aren't capable of protecting them. The killer's voice reinforced his resolve. *You're involved in a game that the academy didn't prepare you for. People's lives are depending on you.*

Zy'kia understood he was in this until the end. Like it or not.

"Like I said in our initial conversation," Captain Winningham's soprano tugged him back inside the office. "I and my team of detectives are willing to assist you in any manner necessary. It is my personal opinion, which isn't worth a pile of beans to anyone other than myself, but I feel you are more than capable of solving these cases. I expressed these sentiments to my superiors when I learned of the possibility of you being removed." Sincerity flowed from Captain Winningham's tone.

"Again, my opinion, but I feel the very idea is an insult, a slap in the face, to someone that has proven himself time and time again. If it does come to you being removed, I'd like for you to remain active on the case. I'd consider it an honor and a privilege to work alongside you, detective." Sheriff Norris nearly fell from his chair. He had been of the opinion that all government men were arrogant jerks.

Captain Winningham leaned forward, extending his right hand. "I sincerely mean every word." He released Zy'kia's hand. "We're employed by different agencies, but we're on the same team."

Major Madison offered his right hand. "We all are," he said while eyeballing Sheriff Norris.

CHAPTER 19

"The death of Senior Airman Felicia Mendez has caused the government to take a special interest in the murderous spree that has plagued Okaloosa County over the last five months." Javid became fixated on his television. "Inside sources say, Sheriff Norris has been given a deadline. The amount of time wasn't disclosed, failure to close the case within the timeframe will automatically forfeit jurisdiction and the government will become the lead agency."

Sounds like the mutt is on his way to the dog pound. Let's adopt a pet, Chip.

Since he doesn't fetch too good, maybe we can teach him to roll over and play dead.

Javid smiled.

"Efforts to contact Sheriff Norris were in vain. His office declined to make a comment but did say a statement will be released later in the week."

Send him some flowers, Chip.

Yeah! Offer him our condolences.

"Mounting concerns have divided the residents of Okaloosa county. Feeling law enforcement isn't doing enough to protect them, vigilante groups are patrolling their neighborhoods. One resident of Overbrook Estates had this message for the murderer." The camera zoomed in for a closeup of the redneck that spoke at the city council meeting.

"Consider us armed and dangerous."

He wore camouflage pants with a Confederate flag T-shirt. The bulge of his pistol was clearly visible in his waistline.

"In area news, authorities have arrested eight men in connection.." Javid muted the television.

Now is the time, Chip.

***

Poppa gazed around the living room of his small apartment. Jose Cuervo bottles littered the coffee table, evidence that his drinking had spiraled out of control.

Visions of Zy'kia's lady friend formed, despite his drunken stupor. *I have to find out who she is*, he thought.

He'd imagined choking the life from her body countless times. Each act was calculated to insure he'd receive the greatest amount of pleasure possible.

He appreciated the images that came next. Those of the great Detective Blunt crying his grief-stricken heart out over her lifeless body. As a way of celebrating, Poppa reached for the half-empty liquor bottle that sat on the floor at his feet.

***

"The spare key is in the third flowerpot from the left on the right side of the walkway. Promise me you'll be safely locked inside before dark." Zy'kia listened as the person on the other line replied.

"I'll be there around eight." He placed the receiver in its cradle ending the call.

Closing his eyes, Zy'kia mentally relived the past six months of his life. He'd refitted the pieces of his puzzle that were thrown out of whack due to his divorce from Kim. His career was on the upswing. Being nominated Officer of the Year testified to that.

Then the murders began. The first two didn't raise any alarms. It was the third that made him realize a problem was on the horizon.

The clue?

A bag of Lays potato chips had been left at all of the crime scenes. The killer's signature.

He was amazed by the carefulness displayed by the killer. And shocked by the manner in which he killed.

Insulin.

Contrary to popular belief, he'd committed the perfect crime repeatedly. He could walk away now and never be caught.

Then the mode of killing changed from insulin to strangulation. It was uncommon for a killer to change the way he committed his chosen crime.

The idea of there being two killers was feasible. Without concrete facts about one killer. There wasn't any way to factually say there were two.

The phone calls intrigued him the most. The killer's arrogant, cocky attitude. The way he viewed killing as a game. Zy'kia knew he was dealing with a very deranged mind.

Rainstorms produce rainbows. His was named, Leslie.Many years had passed since their teenage love, but the feelings remained intact. Under different circumstances, the reuniting of lost love would be considered a fairytale. The kind found within the pages of romance novels.

But the circumstances weren't different, and the book was a murder mystery, not romance.

Zy'kia spent the prior five days contemplating his decision. In order to fully commit to one, he'd have to sacrifice the other. Leslie vs. his job.

The odds of catching the killer were far less than being able to build a lasting relationship with Leslie. His dilemma centered on, choosing Leslie would be the same as admitting defeat. It'd mean the killer outwitted him and all the ugly things he said were true.

Was he willing to say, he wasn't capable of protecting the people? Would his pride prevent him from saying, he was underqualified to keep his sworn oath?

On the other hand, he couldn't choose his job without sacrificing his only true love. The love his heart had yearned for all the years they were separated. Maybe she'll understand and agree to slow down until the case is over.

Was he that selfish? To put his personal desires ahead of what he believed in his heart to be right. He'd made his decision. Right or wrong he'd have to live with it.

CHAPTER 20

Javid squatted in his usual hiding place as spied on Zy'kia's house. His eyes took in a strawberry-red BMW 328i convertible. The words of his horoscope rang inside his head.

Be patient. Persistence will prevail.

Instincts told him to whom the car belonged. A beautiful car for a beautiful woman. The car's personalized license plate confirmed his beliefs. YNV ME.

Zy'kia's Expedition pulled into the driveway next to the BMW. Javid's excitement increased. As did the voices.

It's the hound, Chip! We can kill two birds with one stone.

Javid's night vision binoculars put him in Zy'kia's footsteps as he followed him to the front door. Determined to discover the mystery lady's identity, Javid settled in to wait for her departure.

Be patient. Persistence will prevail. The words from his horoscope made the hard ground a tad bit more comfortable.

"Hey, baby." Leslie greeted Zy'kia at the front door. "Rough day?" She asked after kissing his cheek.

Wouldn't take much to get used to this, Zy'kia thought silently before replying. "Not really. But I feel so worn out for some reason."

Leslie took his left hand in her right. She led him down the hallway. "A hot bath. A good meal. And me!" she did a semi-twirl. "those are the ingredients for a better evening."

She had the ability to help him forget the reality existing on the other side of the front door. He could easily allow himself to get caught up in the fantasy playing out inside his house. A house that Leslie alone could turn into a home.

"Gyps, we need to talk." He said taking a seat on the toilet.

"We can do that after dinner. Right now I'm gonna need you to relax and.."

"No Gyps. It can't wait." Zy'kia insisted.

Leslie turned from the tub. The tone of his voice tipped her off as something being wrong.

"Okay then, Zy." She turned the water off. "Talk."

Zy'kia hadn't said a word. Yet, Leslie's eyes pooled with tears. She knew in her heart that whatever he had to say wasn't going to do any wonders in making her catastrophic day better.

Zy'kia attempted to swallow the lump in his throat. It refused to budge.

"Babe," he paused.

"Please Zy'kia. Don't torture me just to break my heart."

The tears began falling.

"Gyps." He reached for her hand. "I've waited so many years to feel what I've been enjoying these last couple of months. I feel complete. Safe."

"So why end it?" she blurted.

"I'm not trying to end anything. It's just." Zy'kia hesitated to choose the correct words. "Timing. These murders. I have a duty. An obligation that requires my full concentration, and.."

Leslie rose from the side of the tub. She wiped tears from her face saying, "I get it. You don't have to say anything further.

"No Gyps. Let me finish."

She headed for the door. "No Zy'kia. You listen. Here I am sacrificing everything to be with you. My babies included. All I wanted was for you to add me to your life. I wasn't trying to be the main anything. I just wanted a place to fit." She stormed through the bathroom door.

"Gyps wait!" Zy'kia followed in her wake. "You're misunderstanding!"

"No! I understand perfectly!" pain created the pain spilling from her voice. "You have an obligation and so do I." Leslie snatched her purse off of the driftwood coffee table. Zy'kia trailed her wordlessly to the front door.

Tiptoeing, she kissed his left cheek. "Maybe next lifetime, Zy. I'll always love you." Leslie stepped out into the night, closing the door behind her.

What else did you expect? Zy'kia questioned himself feeling a lot worse than he did twenty minutes prior.

***

Javid would have missed her, if not for the chirp of her car alarm being deactivated. His back was turned to the house adhering to nature's call. He'd turned in time to see her moving swiftly along the walkway.

He focused the binoculars on her silhouette gliding through the darkness. The night vision highlighted her beauty.

He noticed the purposeful manner in which she strode. He forced the remainder of his bladder to the ground, gave a quick shake, and a tuck. Then was off sprinting in the direction of his Sentra.

Javid made a left onto Beal Parkway. Three cars separated him from the prize. He watched the BMW swerve in and out of traffic.

How does a beauty queen drive like a madman? A voice inquired.

He stomped the gas pedal. The Sentra strained to make it through the intersection of Beal Parkway and Racetrack Road.

He slowed after mastering a left on Landview Drive. The one car separating them turned into the Country Corner convenience store.

Kill her, Chip! Show the great detective. No one is safe. The voices urged.

Dumb her body on his doorstep.

Unconsciously, Javid ran his hand over the insulin-filled syringe. "I have bigger plans for her," he spoke out loud.

He made a right on Pointedly Lane. The BMW's taillights disappeared as it rounded a curve. He passed in time to see the BMW pulling into a townhouse's driveway.

"1823" Javid read the home's address as he cruised by.

CHAPTER 21

J avid shook the fog from his brain. His dream remained fresh on his mind. It took a minute for him to realize that he was alone, laying in a twin bed that dominated the space of his room.

He'd fallen asleep trying to formulate a plan to utilize his newfound information.

I say we jump her bones first and foremost.

She's worth a life sentence, Chip.

Javid smiled.

He imagined what making love with someone so beautiful would be like. He chased away the thought. He had to stay focused on the task at hand.

Javid drove around the city of Fort Walton in search of a place to carry out his plan. This would be the hardest and most vital aspect of the scheme he'd conjured up.

***

Poppa cringed from the pounding in his head. He was experiencing the worse of many hangovers. He willed himself to the bathroom. Every step caused a painful explosion inside his skull.

He braced himself with his right hand. His eyes closed in relief, as he released the pressure of a full bladder. Visions of her resting peacefully in death invaded the darkness behind his eyelids.

Poppa opened his eyes. He half expected to see her lying at his feet. Her body contorted in odd angles. Shaking the excess urine from his rod, Poppa spoke under the rumble of water swirling inside of the toilet bowl. "Soon my love. We will meet."

***

Zy'kia lounged at his desk with a nasty taste in his mouth. It wasn't the putridness of bad breath. He'd brushed and gargled as he always did. This was the bitter sensation that only a broken heart can manufacture.

The way he and Leslie departed weighed heavily on his mind. His body was present, but his heart and mind hadn't made it to the office.

"Eight days," he consoled himself. "Then you'll be officially removed from the case." The thought wasn't as comforting as he intended.

Zy'kia picked up the phone to call Leslie. Deciding against it, he replaced the phone in its cradle.

You made the bed. Now lie in it.

***

The moment he saw the building. Javid knew he'd found exactly what he'd been searching for. He would have passed it by, if not for the bright red paint advertising the DO NOT ENTER warning.

He studied the building's structure from the parking lot. It was located in the far northern corner of the old Ver-Val Industries complex. A natural tree line obstructed the view from the street.

A makeshift sign advertised Dr. Death's Haunted House in black and silver spray paint. The building possessed hardly any resemblance to the one in his dream, but Javid was positive it'd serve to make his dream come true. He was ready to put his plan into motion.

CHAPTER 22

"Homicide. Detective Blunt." Zy'kia was in a funk. His life seemed to be in a steady downward spiral. In a matter of three days, he'd touched rock bottom.

"Forgive me for disturbing you at work, detective. I. I am in a bit of a quandary." Zy'kia was sure he'd never heard the voice coming through his earpiece.

The man sounded distraught. His words stumbled over his tongue as if he were uncomfortable revealing what was on his mind.

"It's Leslie," Zy'kia sat up straight. His heart plummeted to the soles of his Stacy Adams Easy Walkers. Closing his eyes, he waited for the bomb to drop.

"She was due in court yesterday. No one has seen or heard from her in two days, and I um…I mean we, um…"

"I haven't seen or spoken to Leslie in almost a week." Zy'kia helped.

"Oh? Really?"

The way the man, whom Zy'kia deduced to be Leslie's husband, Ron, spoke those two words harnessed more pain than a swarm of killer bees.

"I thought you all were," Ron paused.

"No Ron. We aren't. This is Ron, isn't it?"

Silence.

"As I said, forgive me, detective."

"Please, call me Zy'kia."

"As you know, I'm Ron. I'm afraid something terrible has happened to her. This is unlike her. She'd never willingly miss calling the children. With all these murders taking place and all."

Ron didn't have to finish his thought Zy'kia had been thinking the same thing

"What should we do? I mean, should I file a missing person report?"

"Have you been by her house?"

"No. I can't because I don't know where she lives. I assumed she lived with you, but obviously not. She refused to tell her mother because she felt she'd tell me." Ron's tone lingered around embarrassment.

"Leave me your contact information. I will give you a call in an hour. Until you hear from me, keep calling her phone!"

***

How can you resist that big booty, Chip?

He's a fag, man! That's how.

Javid regarded the woman. Leslie, she'd said her name was. He'd done everything possible to make her comfortable. The small mattress supporting her body was courtesy of the voices.

"Are you okay? You should really eat the hamburgers. At least drink some water."

Leslie stared up at the old man peering down at her. "Please. Let me go. I won't say a word to anyone. I swear!"

During one of their earlier conversations, he'd explained to her that he wasn't the killer. He'd even apologized for her being in such a stale, musty place. But the decision, nor choice wasn't his to make.

Her eyes took in the Tops bag. Memories of her and Zy'kia patronizing the hamburger joint as teenagers filled her mind. Two teenagers, blinded by puppy love, stuffing bite after bite of the signature big juicy, greasy Tops burger into their mouths strangely enticed a smile.

That seemed so long ago now. In a world far from her nightmarish reality.

How'd id I get myself into this? She wondered.

Her eyes roamed to the leg iron securely clamped around her right ankle. A five-foot chain ran from her leg through metal bars that ran from the floor to the ceiling.

One moment I'm home and the next I'm here. Leslie thought remembering peeping through the peephole to see an elderly man standing outside her door.

"May I help you?" she'd asked through solid oakwood.

"It's my wife. I think she's having a heart attack." Without hesitation, she yanked the door open. Then her world went dark.

"You must keep your strength. If you wish to survive." The old man's voice broke into her thoughts. He held out the Tops bag. "If only a little."

Leslie tried to place his accent. Haiti. Jamaica. Trinidad? All she was certain of was it originated from an island. "Perhaps later," she replied with a slight smile. One that didn't extend further than her lips.

Zy'kia pushed the Expedition to its limits. Sirens and flashing lights parted the sea of cars as if he were Moses. He dreaded what he'd find when he arrived at Leslie's townhouse.

Blaming himself for allowing her to just walk out, he banged his right fist against the steering wheel.

You're not qualified to protect them, detective.

"Got dammit!" Zy'kia screamed into the Expedition's cab.

To keep from creating a scene, he turned off the lights and siren before turning onto Leslie's street. A tingle of relief washed through his being as he spotted her BMW. He swung the Expedition into driveway next to her car and parked.

Zy'kia ran his left hand across the BMW's hood as he walked past.

Cold.

Using his key, flashed. Instead, he opted to ring the doorbell. Stepping onto the porch, he realized neither option would be necessary. The front door was slightly ajar.

135

Training and instincts kicked in. Zy'kia acted on autopilot. His right fetched his service Glock .40 from his ankle holster without him realizing he'd even bent over.

In times of crisis, a trained mind doesn't waste precious seconds thinking. It reacts and counteracts.

Zy'kia jacked a round into the Glock's chamber. He was confident it would counteract any danger that may be waiting on the other side of the door.

***

Jose Cuervo seeped through Poppa's pores. The stench of alcohol was overpowering. Today was day four spent comatose in a drunken state.

"Tu' son mi amigo, Solamente," Poppa spoke reverently to the fresh bottle of Jose Cuervo.

"You are my only friend," he repeated in English.

Poppa used his left palm to pat the bottom of the bottle. It was his belief that he was pushing evil spirits to the top to allow their escape when he opened it.

He once felt the same about Javid. Things had become different between them for reasons beyond his comprehension. They no longer hung out, sharing laughs and conversations. If not for work, they wouldn't see each other.

Imaginations of Javid's eyes bulging, him gasping for air as he choked the life out of him became frequent.

How did we permit many years of friendship to come to this? Poppa broke the seal on the Jose Cuervo.

"Betrayal deserves death," Poppa spoke out loud, pouring alcohol into his glass.

"How is it that the honorable Marines say? Death before dishonor?" Poppa raised his glad in a mock toast. Then he emptied it in one giant gulp.

***

"Her car is in the driveway," Zy'kia relayed the results of his visit to Leslie's townhouse to Ron. "The front door was slightly ajar when I arrived. There weren't any signs of a struggle, but she wasn't anywhere to be found. Nothing of value seemed to be missing, that rules out a burglary." Zy'kia paused to let Ron ask questions.

None came.

"Did she have enemies?" Zy'kia operated in detective mode.

"Leslie? Be for real," Ron's tone hinted at Zy'kia's stupidity for asking the question.

"One of her best friends was found murdered. Now she does the impossible and vanishes in mid-air. I am being for real!" Zy'kia responded heatedly.

Humbled, Ron replied. "No sir. None that I know of. Do you think she's," pause. "dead?" Ron's voice cracked, dreading the possibility.

"Now what I think is, we're going to have to work together to find her. I want you to report her missing. Tell the officer it may be a possible abduction." Zy'kia glanced up to see Officer Curtis standing in his doorway.

He covered the mouthpiece and beckoned Officer Curtis to speak.

"A call came through the tip line when you were out. The caller said you'd understand the meaning." Zy'kia nodded.

"It's urgent, detective." Officer Curtis eyed the phone receiver in Zy'kia's right hand. Then eased the office door closed behind him.

"I have to run, Ron. Follow my instructions and continue to call her phone. I'll contact you later," Zy'kia pressed end and hurried off to see what Curt considered to be urgent.

***

Javid walked away from the payphone smiling. *Wait until he gets a load of that, Chip! That was a grand idea.* The voices congratulated.

And this disguise. Who would have ever thunk it?

Let's go sex her lights out! That's what a dirty old man would do.

I got first. No sloppy seconds for this stud.

This plan is better than any episode of C.S.I.! Let's go get Poppa. He deserves exactly what he'll get for trying to steal our glory!

Chip, my man. I gotta give it to you. I wouldn't want to be on your bad side. That's for sure!

***

"Help, detective! A fox has broken into my hen house and stole my prized hen, Leslie." Zy'kia listened to a recorded call from the tipline for the third time.

"Do you love her, Detective Blunt? If yes, I'll allow you to rescue her, and put an end to the murdering spree." Zy'kia checked Happy. He shrugged his shoulders. Then focused on Officer Curtis, taking Zy'kia's gaze with him.

"As I've said, your seventy-two percent was compiled at the expense of incompetent criminals." Officer Curtis exchanged bewildered looks with the tip line operator who'd taken the call.

"Since we see you aren't capable of catching an old fox. I'll help you, but if you fail." The sinister laugh that Zy'kia despised sent anger chills rippling through his body.

"She dies," the killer went on. "Nice and slow. And that's after I rape every hole on her body. You accomplish the task at hand, and I'll be your reward. The city can once again sing their praises of their beloved Detective Blunt.

Let me tell you how this is going to work. I'll remain with her for twenty-four hours. One second after and her death sentence begins," the killer chuckled.

138

"You want her? Solve this riddle. A simple one for a simple mind. Ready? Here goes.

An apple a day will keep me away. I am not him. Just his messenger. Who am I?

You have twenty-four hours from 2:15 pm today. Not a sad sigh more. Now fetch you sorry excuse for a hound."

Zy'kia checked his trusty Timex, at 2:52 pm. The countdown had begun.

CHAPTER 23

"**D**o you think you could live any fouler than you are?" Javid pinched his nose standing at Poppa's threshold.

"It smells like alcohol and ass in here. And then at least a double dose more of both. What the hell is wrong with you, man?" Javid stopped at the nearest window. He raised it as high as it would go.

Stepping over and around empty liquor bottles, Javid made his way to every window. He opened them all to full capacity.

"Get out and leave me be," Poppa slurred, gulping from a bottle of Tequila.

Disgusted, Javid slapped the bottle from Poppa's hand. It shattered against the floor. Poppa's eyes widened. A mixture of surprise and anger. He looked at his fiery alcohol pooling on the dingy tile and became incensed.

"You black bastard!" he hissed. "Who or what gives you the right to enter my house and act as if you own it?" Poppa swayed on drunken legs.

"Tranquillo amigo. Take it easy. I came to give you the gift of a lifetime. Not to fight with you, my friend. But you must promise not to harm her until I return to watch."

Poppa toweled off beads of water, while downing cups of coffee strong enough to float horseshoes. Clean, but far from sober. Poppa listened as Javid filled him in.

"Are you serious? You did that for me?"

"Especially for you, amigo. If you promise to do as I ask," Javid reminded.

"Sure. I give you, my word. Death before dishonor. I will introduce myself properly, as I wait for you to return. You will permit me a taste to celebrate the occasion, won't you, amigo?" Poppa eyed the lone bottle of Jose Cuervo that miraculously survived Javid's purge. He licked his lips in anticipation.

"I don't care what you do as long as you don't kill her before my return," Javid admonished.

"I will never be able to repay such a kind deed. Thank you again, my friend." Poppa extended his right hand.

Shaking it, Javid replied. "Think nothing of it. That's what friends are for."

4:18 pm., Zy'kia huddled around his desk. Happy and Curt flanked him.

"I do believe. We are making this harder than what it is," Curt admitted for the second time.

"Well, Einstein since it's so easy. What is the answer?" Happy retorted.

Curt didn't bother responding. He'd said, "he felt they were making it hard." Not that he knew the riddle's answer.

"He said, "I can find them with the answer. Wouldn't that mean, the answer has to be a location?" Zy'kia interjected.

"I am thinking along the same lines. I don't know of any places that deal with apples and messengers," Happy offered.

Zy'kia lowered his head. His eyes swept the stationary centered on his desk, reading the riddle time and time again. "My best guess is a hospital." Curt volunteered. "An apple a day will keep the doctor away. His secretary is his messenger," he explained.

"Should we have someone check the hospitals?" Happy stared at Zy'kia for the green light.

"That's a logical theory," Zy'kia agreed. "We're in crisis mode. We're checking out everything we think of. Have someone circulate these also." He passed Happy a stack of photocopies of Leslie's picture.

"I'll get someone right on it." Happy retrieved the pictures saying, "Impossible to forget a face this pretty. Was she really yours once upon a time?"

"Yes. Now get moving! I'd like to see her again. Alive!" Zy'kia hurried Happy on his way.

***

"Remember. You gave me your word." Javid spoke through the Sentra's driver's window. Poppa closed the Mazda's driver's door. "I'll return before 2:15 tomorrow."

Poppa studied Ver-Val Industries' parking lot. "You have my word, amigo. I will only introduce myself and visualize the fun I shall have when you return. I am going to make it a special show for you. It will be beautiful to remember." Poppa said eagerly wanting to see his biggest fantasy.

Javid winked, sliding the Sentra's gearshift into drive, giving Poppa permission to scurry towards the boarded-up entrance to DR. Death's Haunted House.

Poppa navigated his way through the haunted house following Javid's directions. His excitement escalated with every step. He moved like a shark homed in on a blood scent. A flicker of candlelight marked his prize's location.

A low whistle thrilled from Poppa's mouth. "Sweet Santa Maria. You are prettier than I remember. Bonita. Muy Bonita!" Poppa helped himself to a swallow of Tequila.

"Do not be frightened, my love," he spoke into terror-filled eyes staring up at him.

Poppa lowered himself to the mattress, clinging to the Jose Cuervo bottle as if his life depended on it. Leslie shuffled as far away as her chains would allow.

Reaching out to caress her left calf, he warned. "It is unwise to make Poppa angry."

Javid positioned his sleeping bag inside the tree line in Ver-Val Industries' parking lot. He had a clear view of Dr. Death's Haunted House. His night vision binoculars rested within easy reach.

He glanced at his five-dollar Casio wristwatch, 6:25 pm. Expecting Detective Blunt to arrive with the calvary at any time, Javid settled in comfortably for the wait.

You'll probably end up having to call the dumb hound and give him directions. The voices joked.

Anyone with a pea for a brain would have been here by now.

Javid embraced the voices, giving them total access to his mind without resistance. They deserved the treat of the plan he'd masterminded. After all, they played a major role in him being who he was. The slickest fox of them all.

***

"The hospitals were all negatives," Happy closed his cellphone.

"What should I do about the media outside?" He asked peeking through the blinds.

"How in the hell? No. Why in the hell are they out there in the first place?" Zy'kia checked his Timex, 10:11 pm.

"Never mind them. Time is expiring quickly, and we haven't made any progress." Zy'kia's tone was a mixture of pain and irritation.

"An apple a day will keep the doctor away. I am not him. Just his messenger." Zy'kia repeated the riddle out loud, hoping that hearing the words would trigger his brain.

"Could the last half mean? The caller isn't the actual killer. Just his messenger?" Happy wondered.

"How would that tie in with the first part?" Curt refuted. "And what does that have to do with location?"

"Hell, I don't know! I am just as lost as you." Happy testified.

***

"You are more perfect than the other. Gloria, her name was."

Hearing Poppa mention Gloria's name sent chills cascading through her body. The mind-numbing hand of fear gripped her. She knew the man fondling her breasts was Gloria's killer.

Initially, she'd resisted his touch. The production of a large butcher knife convinced her to reconsider.

"Are you afraid of death?" he asked, squeezing her left nipple.

Recoiling, Leslie bobbed her head up and down. *Did Gloria have to endure this humiliation?* She wondered internally.

"Do you trust your detective boyfriend to save you from death?"

"Y…You…You are m…my… my… only boy…boyfriend." Leslie stammered out the words she'd been instructed to say.

Poppa's face lit up. "And you my dear. Will always be my only love." Poppa added, "Until death doeth u part."

CHAPTER 24

"We're in desperate need of help," Curt stormed the officer's break room. "Is anyone in here good at solving riddles?" His eyes rotating spied a petite redhead with her right hand raised.

"I am," she said. That was enough for Curt. He latched on to her left wrist and beelined for Zy'kia's office.

"Riddles are common sense questions, detective." The redhead, Monica, she'd said her name was, sat in a chair next to Zy'kia. "They're usually quite simple to solve if you don't confuse yourself by making it harder than it is."

"That's exactly what I said," Curt sounded as if she'd stolen the answer to a million-dollar question.

"This is a life-or-death situation." She looked like, 'yeah right.' "Literally!" Curt's added force got her attention.

"I need you to take a look at this," Zy'kia slid the stationary to her side of his desk.

"Is this the reason for all of them?" She asked, referring to the horde of media outlets gathered outside.

"Yes. Now if you are done asking questions, I'll appreciate you answering one." Monica met Zy'kia's gaze head-on.

"Sure, detective. Ask away," she responded.

Zy'kia pointed to the stationary. Her eyes dropped and six others focused on her. Breathing became the office's soundtrack.

Five breaths and an exhale later, Monica turned to Zy'kia. A smile bisected her face. "That's easy enough. I remember reading one similar in a magazine called Simple Riddles For Simple Minds." The three men swapped knowing looks. The killer had said as much during his recorded call to the tip line.

145

"It's a two-part riddle," Monica continued. "Where the answers combine to create one."

"You can teach Riddle Solving 101 later, Girlfriend," Happy interrupted. "Right now, we need an answer sweetheart."

"Dr. Death."

"What?" Happy asked confused.

"You were just jumping down my throat for an answer. I gave it to you, and you are still acting crazy. Dr. Death. That is the riddle's answer, boyfriend." She added with a triple shot of attitude.

"Are you sure?" Curt questioned, escorting Monica to the door.

"Positive," she replied an eyeblink before the door slammed in her face.

"Hey!" Happy became animated. "I know of a Dr. Death's Haunted House! It's closed now, but I used to curse having to wait for the line of cars trying to get into the parking lot.

It's in Industrial Park. At the back of the old Ver-Val building. When I think about it…that's a perfect place to…" Happy wasn't allowed to finish his statement. Zy'kia was off and running.

***

3:38 am. Here comes the excitement, Chip!

Damn! Looks like he brought every hound in the kennel.

A convoy of police cruisers converged on the parking lot with their lights off.

Poppa won't make it out of here.

Javid reached for his night vision binoculars. He was afforded a close-up view of the action.

I wonder if he molested her.

If he did, he won't molest anyone else.

That grade A piece is worth going to jail for.

No female is worth dying for. The voices began bickering.

Javid searched the sea of officers spilling from their cruisers. Detective Blunt was missing.

Maybe he's at the vet, Chip.

Yeah, when you broke his heart, they found a worm in it. The voices began to laugh, returning them to one accord.

Javid had learned enough about Detective Blunt to know that nothing short of death would prevent him from being there.

There he is! Over there. Upfront, wagging his tail.

Javid's eyes bounced from officer to officer until they rested on Zy'kia, moving his arms in what Javid guessed to be hand signals.

They're surrounding the place.

It's called setting up a perimeter.

Duh! I watch C.S.I., too.

***

"I repeat. Attention all units. We're going dark. No lights. No sirens." Zy'kia spoke into the Expedition's CB radio. "Remember this is a hostage situation. The suspect is to be taken alive...if possible." He led a convoy of police cruisers as they turned onto Industrial Avenue.

"Teams four and five. I want y'all to take the further most quadrant," Zy'kia issued instructions. "Four to the northeast. Five. Northwest. Arc out until you connect. And let nothing, Absolutely nothing get past you," he faced Happy.

"Guess you'll be receiving a promotion. Team two takes the southeast. Three is on the southwest," Zy'kia barked out orders.

"Team one. You're with me here in the parking lot," Zy'kia hung the microphone over the Expedition's gearshift.

He watched from his driver's seat as teams two through five exited their vehicles.

"Team five in position." The CB crackled to life.

"Team four, set." Adrenaline increased Zy'kia's heart rate.

"Teams two and three. Ready sir."

"Perimeter secured. Northeast to the northwest." A voice announced.

147

"10-4." Zy'kia opened his door.

"All positions hold until my call. Team one. We're up!" He dropped the mic and scrambled into the darkness.

***

Poppa sniffed at the moisture clinging to his fingers.

"Ah, the fragrance of love." He tasted the stickiness. "The taste is even more tantalizing than the scent. This emotion called love is a beautiful thing, no?"

Leslie lay on the mattress, naked as the day she arrived. Tears streamed through closed eyelids.

"Please do not cry my beautiful. It upsets me to think that you are not happy," Poppa twirled several of her locks around his left index finger. Is that what you want? To make Poppa upset?"

Leslie opened her eyes to find Poppa inches from her face. She recoiled faster than a diamondback. Then shivered.

She was greeted by a coldness she believed only existed in movies.

Lord have mercy! She silently prayed.

Thoughts of her family flashed through her skull. She wondered what it must have been like for Gloria.

Was she also degraded and humiliated in her final hours?"

"Come taste the love Poppa has for you," Reality struck like twin lightning bolts. Poppa stood caressing his swollen shaft.

Feeling as if she couldn't withstand it anymore, Leslie considered refusing his request; accepting whatever consequences fate had in store.

We choose our destinies. Her grandmother's voice echoed inside her head. *Think of your babies. You can overcome anything he does to your body. You cannot overcome death!*

Leslie accepted the situation for what it was. She closed her eyes and lowered her head towards reality.

***

Zy'kia's jacking a round into his Glock .40 sent the voices clamoring.

Poppa's bout to get messed up big time!

Hey Poppa! Kill yourself! A roar of laughter filled Javid's head. The voices were being thoroughly entertained.

Javid witnessed the scene unfolding in the parking lot before him. Impressed, he gained a newfound respect for Zy'kia. He decided it wouldn't be fair to hold Zy'kia's inability to apprehend him against him.

We're slicker than the average fox, Chip! Give the poor fella a break.

How'd I miss that? Zy'kia spotted an old Mazda Pickup truck in the back of the parking lot. It required a second look and a head scratch for him to place the truck across the street from his house. The truck seemed to increase in significance the longer he looked at it.

"I'm going in," Zy'kia informed his comrades.

"We'll back you," Happy spoke for himself and Curt.

Inching his way along a wall through the darkness, Zykia followed the faint glow of a light shining in the back of the building.

His nerves were on edge. His mind hinted for him to rush forward to rescue Leslie from God only knows what she must be sustaining. Training advised otherwise. He forced himself to remain patient and exercise extreme caution.

A man's gruff rumble reverberated off the walls into the hallway where Zy'kia crouched.

"This emotion called love is a beautiful thing, no?"

He leaned forward in an attempt to peer inside the room. "Please do not cry my beautiful. It upsets me to think you are not happy," the voice continued.

Immediately Zy'kia recognized the voice as not being the same as the one badgering him over the phone. And it wasn't the voice that left the riddle on the tipline.

149

"Is that what you want? To upset Poppa?"

Zy'kia tried placing the speaker in an exact location and use that information to predict where the second person would be.

He knew when he entered every decision will be made in a split second. Neutralizing the suspect was the agenda.

"Come taste the love Poppa has for you." The Spanish accent told of the speaker's heritage. He uploaded the faces of the men working on the driveway across from his house.

One black. One Latino.

Knowing time was precious, Zy'kia held up three fingers.

Then two.

Then one.

Zy'kia rocketed into the room. His danger counteractor led the charge.

***

Poppa watched with extreme anticipation, as her head crept closer to his throbbing member.

He twitched.

Her soft hands wrapped around him. He felt the warmth of her breath. Then all hell broke loose.

"Don't move another fuckin' muscle!" The voice reached Poppa at the end of rushing footsteps.

Poppa opened his eyes to find himself being bird dogged by the scariest-looking gun he'd ever seen.

The dark eye of death He thought.

He wasn't conscious of the fact that she no longer held him in her hands. Something had gone wrong. His mind froze. Brain cells malfunctioned. His wildest fantasy transformed into his worst nightmare.

Leslie scampered as far from Poppa as her chains would allow. The sound of them scraping across the floor didn't register to him.

Finally, able to think past the gun's one eye. Poppa recognized the terrifying grimace grilling him to belong to the black detective. Zy'kia Blunt.

Poppa's eyes darted in the direction of the butcher knife that lay on the floor beyond his reach.

"Please. I'm begging you. Try it." Poppa noticed the two white officers for the first time.

Angels of Death he surmised.

"I surrender," Poppa whispered.

He eyed Leslie standing in the distance taking it all in. Too much in shock to cover her nakedness.

"Put it down, Zy'kia. It's over." Curt said, kicking the knife away.

Seeing the amount of pressure being applied to the gun's trigger, Poppa realized the extent of the danger facing him. He leaned closer to the officer handcuffing him.

"Put it down, Zy'kia. He isn't worth it." Curt's words fell on deaf ears.

"I am crazy, amigo. I need help." A thankful relief flooded through Poppa's pores, as the gun slowly began to lower. Empowered by the sight, he continued. "I want to go where the crazy people are. Do you hear me, amigo? I am crazy."

Magically, the gun returned to stare him in the eyes. "I'll send you where you belong," Poppa heard the statement but wasn't given the time to comprehend it. His head slammed back onto the mattress, driven by two .40 caliber slugs.

***

Zy'kia rushed into the room to find Leslie holding a man's penis in the process of performing oral sex. The element of surprise combined with the man having his eyes closed gave Zy'kia total control of the situation from the onset.

"Don't move another fuckin' muscle!" On autopilot, Zy'kia hardly realized he'd spoken.

151

The sound of steel dragging across the building's concrete slab registered, as Leslie scurried away. Zy'kia looked down. What he saw ignited a hatred he didn't know existed within him.

An iron leg shackle clamped around her ankle is what fueled the anger flowing inside. Zy'kia peered through his Glock's sights into the face of evilness.

He searched hard for a reason not to pull the trigger. Seeing the man eyeballing the knife on the floor, Zy'kia prayed God would give him the courage to reach for it.

"Please. I'm begging you. Try it." Zy'kia offered encouragement realizing God wasn't going to intervene.

"Put it down Zy'kia. He isn't worth it." Curt's words fell on deaf ears.

I can't Zy'kia thought applying pressure to the trigger. *What about the lives he took? The families he's affected. I can't put it down* his gaze drifted to Leslie.

The sight of her being chained like an animal broke his heart and canceled any understanding he may have had.

"I am crazy, amigo. I need help." Poppa's smirk blew Zy'kia's final fuse. "I want to go to where the crazy people are. Do you hear me, amigo? I am crazy."

Zy'kia envisioned Poppa walking out of the courtroom due to a legal technicality. His mind played a scene of his graduation from the academy. His right hand raised, as he swore an oath to serve and protect.

You're in a game, detective. A fox hunt.

This is far from a game Zy'kia conceded.

Comes a time in life where you have to be willing to die for what you believe in. His father's voice broke through.

In times of crisis, a trained body doesn't think. It reacts and counteracts. Zy'kia's Glock leveled at Poppa's head.

Exhibit A: a trained body reacting.

"I'll send you where you belong."

The Glock translated. It jumped twice in Zy'kia's right hand.

Exhibit B: a counteractor at work.
Two .40 caliber slugs beat Poppa back onto the mattress.
Exhibit C: Justice.

CHAPTER 25

"In the wee hours, Fort Walton Beach Police, led by Detective Zy'kia Blunt led a raid on Dr. Death's Hunted House," a file picture of the haunted house filled the television's screen.

The picture changed to show the bright red sign advertising; Do Not Enter!

The news reporter continued, "Anonymous sources say, the police received a tip from the tip line that led them to this location.

The tip came in the form of a riddle, which authorities believe came from the killer himself. Who was pronounced dead at the scene," A gurney carrying Poppa's corpse rolled across the screen.

"Police were forced to use deadly force when the suspect, who has yet to be identified, attacked officers with this large butcher knife," The knife claimed its five seconds of fame.

"A woman, whose identity is being withheld was heroically rescued during the raid. If not for the courage and bravery displayed, she could have easily been this morning's top story.

"Authorities are using DNA samples to determine how many, if any, of the eleven murders that have gripped Okaloosa County can be attributed to last night's suspect. When asked for a statement, Detective Blunt had this to say,"

The cameras showed Zy'kia leading Leslie from the building to a waiting ambulance. Her face burrowed into his chest, keeping her identity a mystery.

"The suspect has been neutralized. At this time, we have reasons to believe he is responsible for at least some of the murders that have transpired over the last few months.

We'll continue to investigate until we have placed all the pieces in their proper places.

I'd like to use this moment to announce my retirement. I'm hereby giving my two weeks' notice and taking a leave of absence. All effective immediately."

The cameras returned to Sue Vaughn in the studio. "The detective's retirement shocked the entire law enforcement community. He provided a form of closure for the victims' families. As a result, these three officers will receive promotions." Happy, Curt, and Monica were all smiles when the cameras captured them.

"Detective Gilmore will be promoted to head detective, replacing Detective Blunt. Officer Craig Curtis will be promoted to detective first grade and Officer Monica Brown will become patrolwoman Brown, upgrading from her position as traffic guard.

In case you missed it in the opening, Fort Walton Beach Police have killed a suspect they believe to be responsible for the murders that have plagued Okaloosa County over the past three months. I'm Sue Vaughn and this been a special edition of W.E.A.R. Channel Three news."

Javid used the television's remote to turn the TV off. *This is better than C.S.I., Chip.*

Let's call an escort.

Celebration time, come on! The voices began singing Kool and the Gang's hit song 'Celebration'.

Escort? A five-dollar crackhead will do! Just get some sex, man!

Javid agreed. Executing his plan to perfection deserved a celebration. He grumbled to his feet under the voices' applause.

In his bedroom, he flopped on his box spring bed and flipped the phonebook to the yellow pages, and began searching under E, for escort.

***

Two Years Later

"Your breakfast will be ready before you return from getting the morning paper," Leslie called out from the kitchen.

She and Zy'kia were enjoying a weekend alone. The children were with Ron.

Zy'kia slipped his feet into his Pierre Cardin slippers. He stepped over the front door's threshold to a crunch under his foot.

Another step. Another crunch.

Looking down, he drew a sharp intake of breath. The feeling flowing within made the experience similar to being punched in the gut. His eyes followed a trail of potato chips the length of the walkway.

Zy'kia renewed his trek to retrieve the morning edition of the Playground Daily News. He struggled to steady his breath. *This can't be true! It can't...*

He stopped short. Tongue-tied by a slip of paper tucked beneath his Expedition's left windshield wiper blade.

How? He wondered.

He was living his best life. He and Leslie were celebrating their second wedding anniversary, today.

Ron hadn't pursued his custody battle, believing Leslie had been through enough already.

He'd been hired as the head basketball coach of Fort Walton High School. This upcoming season would be his first.

The City of Fort Walton had given him the Expedition as a token of appreciation for his services. Everyone agreed no one else would look right driving it.

His right hand trembled through the air on its way to pluck the slip of paper from the windshield wiper's grasp.

Nervously dreading the outcome of what he knew couldn't be good, Zy'kia braced himself against the Expedition's body. Two

156

and a half tons of support, and still he felt he needed more as he read three words...

READY TO PLAY?

Made in the USA
Columbia, SC
21 February 2023

12727036R00089